ROBERTA LEIGH

cupboard love

Harlequin Books

TORONTO • LONDON • NEW YORK • AMSTERDAM • SYDNEY • WINNIPEG

Harlequin Presents edition published December 1976
ISBN 0-373-70669-3

Original hardcover edition published in 1976
by Mills & Boon Limited

Printed in Canada

CHAPTER ONE

'YOUR father and I would feel much happier if you came with us to Kuwait,' Mrs. Jones reiterated to her daughter Miranda. 'Most girls would jump at the chance.'

'For a holiday, maybe,' Miranda replied, 'but not for two years.'

'You needn't stay if you don't like it.'

'No, Mother.' Miranda pushed a long strand of black hair away from her forehead. 'This little pigeon wants to leave the nest, and Barbara's offer is exactly what I've been looking for.'

'But she's so worldly and——'

'If she weren't, you'd use that as an excuse too,' Miranda said impatiently. 'If I'm going to live with another girl, surely it's better if she's someone who knows her way around rather than a young innocent?'

'When you put it like that,' Mrs. Jones said doubtfully, 'I suppose you're right.'

Miranda saw the reply as a final submission. Had she been less kind-hearted she would have taken the bit between her teeth long ago, but it was difficult to be obstreperous when one had parents who did everything they could to give you what you wanted—short of personal freedom. But now at last even that was imminent, and she longed to fling out her arms in joy, only refraining because her mother might start to wonder what horrifying things she planned to do when she was finally left alone.

'Your father will put extra money into your bank account,' Mrs. Jones was speaking again. 'Then if you don't like working for Barbara, you can fly out to join us.'

'I'm sure I'll like working with her. It's a great chance for me, Mummy.'

Mrs. Jones sighed. 'When we agreed to let you go to Madame Elise we didn't see you becoming a professional cook. We only saw it as being a great advantage for you when you married.'

'Oh, it *will* be,' Miranda assured her, 'and it will be a great advantage for me while I'm single too.'

Forestalling any further comment, Miranda gave her mother a hug, silently counting the days until their Kensington flat was closed and she could move in with her friend. Barbara had little time for worrying parents: an orphan brought up by an unloving cousin, she had, over the past four years, carved out a highly successful career for herself.

'My cousin only sent me to Madame Elise,' Barbara had once told her, 'because she wanted to train me to be a cook-housekeeper for her. When Madame asked me to stay on as her assistant, I thought heaven had come down to earth!'

It was during Barbara's time as a teacher at the school that Miranda had come there, and though she did not have Barbara's flair as a cook, she was considerably better than average. The two girls had remained friends even after Miranda had qualified, and six months later Barbara had also left the school, though in her case it had been to start her own business. Six months after that had come a call for Miranda to join her.

'I employ two other girls and we go to three companies in the City and cook lunches for the directors. I need someone else to help me, so how about it?'

Without any hesitation Miranda had said yes, not knowing at the time that her parents would be going abroad for two years and that Barbara, learning this, would give Miranda the opportunity of sharing her own flat.

'Will you have to wear a uniform?' Mrs. Jones' question brought Miranda back to the present.

'Only an apron and a band round my hair to stop it

6

falling over the food.'

'It's going to be awfully hard work.'

'I'll be finished every day at three,' Miranda said firmly. 'Anyway, I'm as fit as a flea!'

She postured her five feet two inches in front of her mother. Below average in height, she was also delicately built and had an ethereal quality that contrasted sharply with her dramatic colouring of creamy skin, coal-black hair—thick and silky and worn away from her face—and wide-apart aquamarine eyes. Her eyes were her most noticeable feature, being large and tilted at the corners, which gave her a provocative look at variance with her blunt and straightforward nature.

'You don't need to worry about my overworking,' she reasserted. 'With Madame Elise's training behind me I can easily cope with directors' lunches.' She put her hands on her hips. 'Miss Supercook at your service! You might as well take advantage of me while you're still here and let me cook dinner for you tonight.'

Mrs. Jones smiled. 'I must admit it's an advantage having a domesticated daughter—even though I'm not going to accept your offer. Your father and I want to take you out for a farewell celebration.' There was a heavy sigh. 'This time next week I'll be living in a company house looking out on an oil field—again.'

'You know you'll love the life once you're there. All those bridge afternoons and gossipy hen parties!'

'Show more respect for my grey hairs,' Mrs. Jones chided.

'I can't respect what you haven't got.'

'Make sure your behaviour doesn't give them to me!'

'With Barbara to watch over me, I'm stuck on the straight and narrow,' Miranda said solemnly. 'She's a sight more bossy than you!'

*

'All yours,' Barbara Gould said, waving her arm around the room into which she had just shown Miranda. 'You'll be completely your own boss.'

Miranda chuckled, remembering what she had said to her mother a week ago.

'What's the joke?' Barbara asked.

'Just pleasure at being treated like a grown-up at last.'

'Why shouldn't you be? You're over twenty-one—though I must say you don't look it. It's because you're so slight and have that mass of dark hair.' Barbara pointed to a cupboard. 'If it isn't big enough for your clothes, I can let you have another one in the hall.'

'This will be ample.' Miranda bent to the floor and opened one of her cases. 'I'm very tidy, you know, and if things are put away properly they don't take up so much room.'

'You are tidy and capable,' Barbara agreed, 'though you're lucky you don't look it.'

'Lucky?' Miranda queried.

'Sure. Men don't like capable girl-friends—only capable wives.'

'You have to be a girl-friend first.'

'Remember to be a helpless one.' Barbara opened the door. 'I'll leave you to put your things away. Join me in the sitting room when you've finished.'

An hour later Miranda did so, thinking nostalgically of her parents thousands of miles away from her, and of the new life which she herself was embarking upon.

'Tell me about the work I'll be doing,' she said, pushing away a surprising desire to feel homesick.

'I already have.' Barbara ran a hand through her curly brown hair. She was a big-boned girl with a brusque manner which hid a warm nature. She was also highly competent and the cookery company she had started a short while ago had already done well enough for her to buy a small van. 'We cook lunches for three firms in the City. A small property company, a merchant bank and a solicitor's office.'

'I thought only big firms had their own lunch rooms?'

'A small one can also find that it pays,' Barbara explained, 'especially if they have the space for a dining room and kitchen. When you consider what it costs to eat out, as well as the time it takes to get there and back from a restaurant, it's cheaper to have people like us laying everything on for them. We order all the food and make sure the kitchen runs without any problems. Once a week each company gives us a list of the guests they'll be inviting and we plan the menus and submit them for approval.'

'To the boss?'

Barbara shook her head. 'I've never seen the boss in any of the companies. One of the directors is put in charge of the catering and we deal with him if there's anything special to discuss. But generally it's the butler who makes the arrangements.'

'I didn't realise we'd have butlers. At least it makes it easier for serving.'

'My cooks never serve,' Barbara said forcefully. 'We provide elaborate meals, Miranda, and we're busy in the kitchen the whole time. The law firm and the property company have a butler and waitress, and the merchant bank has a butler and waiter. Anyway, you don't need to worry about that for the moment. Your concern during the next few months is buying the food.'

'I have a horrible feeling that's the most unwanted job!'

'It is, if you like snoozing in bed,' Barbara grinned. 'You have to be up at the crack of dawn if you want to get the best fruit and vegetables.'

'Really at the crack of dawn?'

'I'm teasing you. If we were running a shop we'd have to be there at six, but for our line of business, seven-thirty is fine. I've found a few good wholesalers and I stick with them. The amount of stuff I buy isn't worth the hassle of getting there at dawn.'

'Amen,' Miranda said fervently, and Barbara grinned again.

'I'll come with you the first couple of days and introduce you around. Once you're known, you'll be treated right.'

'I suppose we save a lot of money by going direct to the markets?'

'About fifty per cent,' Barbara said, 'and that means more profit for us. I charge the companies for the food at normal retail prices!'

'No wonder you can afford a van!'

'The men we cook for drive Rolls-Royces!'

'I still wouldn't change my job for theirs.'

'One day I'll be driving a Rolls too,' Barbara said seriously. 'Well, maybe not a Rolls but its equivalent.' Her brown eyes gleamed. 'You didn't know I was so ambitious, did you?'

'No, I didn't.' Miranda stood up. 'I just like a job that I enjoy doing. I suppose I *will* get a chance to do some cooking eventually?'

'Of course. We take it in turns to do the shopping stint. I've just finished a three-month one and you'll be taking over from me.'

'You mean I'll be cooking in three months?'

Barbara nodded. 'You'll take over my Mary or Joan.'

'Don't the companies mind having a different cook? I mean, if they get used to one person——'

'You have to make notes of the directors' preferences. In that way, any one of us can step in and take over without there being a fuss. Don't worry, Miranda, it works very well; my success proves it.'

In the next month Miranda appreciated how large Barbara's success was, for two recommendations, one from the law firm and one from a man who had lunched several times at the merchant bank, brought them two more City lunch rooms who required a cook. This meant engaging two extra cooks and gave Miranda a bigger shopping list to fulfil, which in turn meant increasing the profit.

For the first week it had been an agony to get up at six o'clock, but once her system became used to it, she awoke automatically. The wholesalers quickly got to know her and she found her appearance an asset and never had any shortage of volunteers to help carry her purchases to the van. One glance from her aquamarine eyes always brought someone eager to lift the baskets or boxes. She went twice a week to buy fresh fish, but only bought fresh meat once a fortnight, storing sufficient in the vast freezer which Barbara kept in the basement lumber room that belonged to her flat.

Apart from making her daily purchases, Miranda was responsible for their delivery to each kitchen, and this she found the most temper-fraying task of all, for it frequently meant parking several hundred yards from her destination and carrying the produce the rest of the way by foot. Only at the merchant bank could she rely on assistance, for there was always a commissionaire to help her carry her packages. He was a cheery middle-aged man, always ready with a joke until one morning, five weeks after Miranda had begun her job, when he met her at the steps with a look of anxiety.

'I've been watching out for you,' he said. 'Your friend here has been taken ill.'

'What's wrong with her?'

'Dunno. I was just told not to let you drive off again when you arrived this morning.'

Miranda jumped out of the van. 'I'll go to the kitchen and see what's happened. If you could just make sure I don't get a parking ticket.'

'I'll take it round to our car park,' the commissionaire said, and climbed in as Miranda hurried into the building. She had only been inside the merchant bank once—before she had arranged with the commissionaire to collect the produce from her—and she had to ask the way to the kitchens, finding them to be on the top floor and overlooking an inner courtyard. Mary Robinson, who had trained at Madame Elise's with Barbara, was nowhere to be seen, though at Miranda's entrance a young man in a blue and white striped apron came forward.

'I'm Bert,' he said, 'Mr. Judd's assistant and part-time vegetable boy! Miss Gould left a message for you to ring her as soon as you arrived. The phone's over there.'

'Where is Miss Robinson?' Miranda asked as she dialled Barbara's number.

'One of the directors drove her to the hospital an hour ago. Appendicitis, I think. Either that, or she was pregnant!'

Miranda gave him a cold stare and turned to the telephone as Barbara came on the line to tell her that Mary was, at this moment, being operated on for suspected peritonitis.

'You'll have to stay and take over,' Barbara added. 'I wish it was any place other than the bank.'

'Why?' Miranda's heart gave an unpleasant thump. 'Are they difficult to cater for?'

'Half the directors there consider themselves to be gourmets—with an accent on the word consider.'

'I'm sure I can manage,' Miranda said, not feeling at all sure. 'Anyway, the menus are worked out, so I'll just follow them.'

'It's such a relief having you,' Barbara breathed, 'but if you get into trouble don't hesitate to call me.'

'I won't need to call you,' said Miranda. 'I'll see you tonight.' She put down the telephone and turned to Bert, who had been listening with undisguised interest.

'I can help you, miss,' he said. 'I know all the ropes.'

'Well, make sure I don't trip over them.' Miranda unbuttoned the jacket of her suit. 'I don't suppose Miss Robinson left her apron here, did she?'

'She never even had a chance to put it on.' Going to the cupboard, he took out a white nylon overall and headband. 'The ladies' cloakroom is on the other side of the corridor. Miss Robinson used to change and leave her things there.'

'Then I'll do the same.' Miranda grabbed hold of the things and went out.

She returned looking overwhelmed by Mary's apron, which was a foot too long and flapped unbecomingly around her ankles. She had managed to belt it tightly by the judicious use of safety pins, though lumpy folds bulged around her hips and made her look like a mobile tent.

'Small, ain't you?' Bert grinned.

'But determined,' Miranda said. 'Now how about showing me where everything is kept and also the menu that Miss Robinson had planned for today.'

Bert obligingly took her on a tour of the kitchen. The appliances were modern and there seemed to be many of them, as well as adequate working tops and all the necessary utensils. The menu was written out on a black slate that hung on the wall, and below it in a drawer was a book with the menus for the following week.

'Miss Robinson had just re-checked all the menus with Judd,' said Bert. 'He's the butler.'

Miranda glanced through the book before closing the drawer. She would take it home with her tonight and study the menus. Though Barbara expected her cooks to follow Madame Elise's cooking course, the girls were sufficiently creative to devise some recipes of their own, and if Mary had done this, then Miranda wanted to make sure she knew how to follow them.

But today at least there was no problem. Because it was Friday, Mary had kept to fish. It was a bit too fishy for Miranda's personal taste, but it was too late to change it. Prawn cocktail was followed by crab quiche and salad, and there were two sweets to conclude: hazelnut torte and peaches in Grand Marnier sauce. The first thing was to make the hazelnut cake, then prepare the pastry for the quiche and give it a chance to settle, during which time she could set out the individual prawn cocktails.

'Could you let me have the dishes for the first course,' she asked Bert. 'Then I'll get them ready and put them in the refrigerator.'

'Right,' he said, and proceeded to do so.

'How many are there for lunch?' she called.

'Fourteen.' He turned from the cupboard. 'Sorry, fifteen. Mr. Jefferson is back.'

'Who's he?'

'Big Brother. The Managing Director of the bank.' Bert's voice was mockingly deferential. 'He wasn't due back till the end of next week, but he blew in this morning, noisy as a hurricane and twice as destructive!'

'Destructive?' said Miranda, not concentrating on what was being said as she set out butter and flour on the marble-topped pastry table.

'Well, he's the boss,' Bert explained, 'and everyone jumps like mad when he's around. You know how it is.'

'I'm afraid I don't,' Miranda admitted cheerfully as she mixed the fat with the flour. 'In my kind of job we're our own boss. If I——' she stopped speaking as the commissionaire came into the kitchen carrying the rest of her vegetables and fruit. 'How kind of you,' she beamed. 'I was thinking I would have to go down and fetch them myself.'

'A little thing like you?' the man replied. 'With so many hefty men around there's no call for you to do any fetching and carrying.'

Nodding cheerily, he went out, and Miranda set the pastry to cool in the refrigerator and continued with the rest of her preparations. It was always nerve-racking to work in a kitchen one did not know and Madame Elise's training stood her in good stead, when nerves might otherwise have got the better of her.

At twelve o'clock Judd came in to say that Mary Robinson had had her operation and was as well as could be expected. He was totally different from Bert: quiet and silver-haired and more like a director of the bank than its butler.

'Quite a turn Miss Robinson gave us,' he commented. 'Getting on with her work without any fuss and then suddenly doubling up like a jack-knife.'

'It's a good thing she was taken ill during the day and not in the middle of the night,' said Miranda.

'And a good thing you were able to step in and take her place, if you don't mind my saying so.' Judd moved majestically over to the refrigerator and poured himself a glass of milk. 'Staff don't have their lunch until after the main dining room,' he explained, 'that way we can polish off any left-overs!'

'Is there a staff dining room?' Miranda asked.

'There are only three of us,' Judd explained, 'and we eat in here. If there are a lot of guests—more than fifteen or so—then Mrs. Judd comes down and lends a hand in the kitchen.'

'I think you would need an extra pair of hands in the dining room too.'

'I have Bert,' said Judd. 'When he remembers himself he can be quite good.'

Bert pulled a face at him and then glanced at his watch. 'Have you set out the drinks, Mr. Judd?'

15

'Naturally.' The butler spoke to Miranda. 'Miss Robinson always prepared a tray of canapés. If you haven't had time to do it——'

'I haven't done so because nobody told me they were wanted.'

She dived towards the refrigerator and hurriedly set to work. She was as quick as she was competent, her fingers flashing as she peeled and cut and chopped, then, pink of cheek, she presented a filled silver platter to the admiring butler.

'I can see why your firm is called Superchefs,' he smiled. 'There are no flies on *you*.'

'There should never be flies on a good cook,' Miranda smiled back, and stood on one leg to ease her other one. The one thing she had not come prepared with was a pair of flat-heeled shoes, and rushing round the kitchen for several hours in high heels had given her cramp. She slipped off her shoes and enjoyed the coolness of the tiled floor on the soles of her feet. The cramp miraculously ceased and she pushed her shoes under the table and padded round without them, arousing a startled question from Bert who wanted to know why she had suddenly shrunk.

'I've worn myself to the bone,' she chuckled as she bent to look in the oven. The tops of the quiches were bubbling gently and the aroma of crab, mushroom and Gruyère cheese filled the kitchen.

'This smell is making me hungry,' she murmured.

'Better not let it get out of the kitchen,' said Bert, and dived for a switch on the wall. Immediately there was a soft hum and the faint haze surrounding the two ovens began to disappear. 'Air-conditioning,' he explained. 'I forgot to switch it on earlier. One thing Mr. Jefferson can't stand is the smell of cooking coming into the dining room. It really makes him blow his top.'

Miranda was too concerned with preparing the salad to

pay much attention to what Bert was saying, though she could not help remarking that everything said so far about the Lothian Bank's managing director had not endeared him to her. A noisy hurricane who blew his top at the appetising smell of food was not the sort of person to appeal to a graduate of Madame Elise's school of cookery. She squeezed a lemon, added it to the oil in the small bowl in front of her and then tasted it. A dash more salt and pepper and it would be an ideal vinaigrette. She peeped at the wall clock. Twelve thirty-five. She was well ahead of schedule.

'You'd better be off, Bert,' she warned, 'or Judd will be calling for you.' She saw that the young man was already divesting himself of his apron. In a white linen jacket above dark trousers he looked every inch the professional waiter, especially now that his grin had been replaced by a solemn expression.

'I'll come back in five minutes before everyone sits down,' he warned. 'It's supposed to be at one-fifteen, but you'd better give them an extra few minutes.'

'That's no problem,' Miranda said. 'The first course is cold and the rest won't be spoiled.'

Alone in the kitchen she was too nervous to sit down and rest and made unnecessarily fussy changes to the dishes of prawn cocktail as she took them out of the refrigerator and carefully wiped off any specks of moisture from the plates. Not sure if Bert would return to set them out on the dining room table or whether she herself was expected to do so, she waited for five minutes and, when he did not return, put the dishes on a trolley and wheeled them across the carpeted hall. The dining room was empty, but the door leading to the room beyond was ajar and she heard voices and the clink of glasses, as well as breathed the aroma of cigarettes and cigars. Cigars before lunch: no gourmets here!

'Glad you got back early, Mr. Jefferson,' a thin voice said. 'I thought you were still in New York.'

'It was Houston, actually—a world of its own.' The words were crisp and the voice faintly impatient, as if the man speaking them knew he was just making conversation and resented it.

Having set out all the dishes Miranda quickly retreated and, as she closed the door, glimpsed the far one opening wider and dark-suited men moving into the dining-room. Back in the kitchen she took the quiches from the oven to give them a chance to cool slightly and set before being served. There were four in all, more than enough for everyone to have second helpings should they wish it, and four teak bowls of salad, each one seasoned differently, but all of them combining a tangy mixture of cress, lettuce, carrots and tomatoes to offset the richness of the entrée. She bent to sprinkle fresh basil lightly over one salad, and the white band on her hair slipped forward. Like the apron, it was too big for her and though she had kept it in position by a couple of clips it was uncomfortable and not satisfactory. It slipped again and impatiently she moved away from the table and took it off. Pulling her hair completely away from her face, she used the white band to tie it into a ponytail, then she returned to the table and sprinkled finely grated chocolate over the cream that masked the hazelnut torte. It was a rich and luscious concoction of powder-fine hazelnuts whipped into a sponge mixture, and the accompanying dish of peaches added piquancy to something that might otherwise have been too sweet. Miranda tasted the cream from the cake. She had a sweet tooth and could easily have sat down and demolished half of it there and then. What consternation there would be in the dining room if she did! With a flourish she placed the gateau on a superb crystal dish and set it aside.

'Ready for the next lot,' Bert said in a low tone as he wheeled in a trolley piled with empty dishes and wheeled out the second trolley with the quiches.

18

Miranda piled the dishes into the dishwasher and saw that one prawn cocktail had not been touched. She made a face and pushed it down the waste disposal unit, turning as she heard a step behind her and saw Judd, a look of agitation on his face.

'Oh dear,' he muttered. 'It quite slipped my mind to tell you.'

'About what?'

'Mr. Jefferson being back. I mentioned it to Miss Robinson, of course, but when she collapsed it went out of my head and I never thought to tell *you*.'

'It didn't matter,' Miranda assured him. 'Bert told me.'

'But he didn't tell you that Mr. Jefferson is allergic to fish.'

Miranda remembered the uneaten prawn cocktail. 'Oh dear.' Then she remembered the crab quiche. 'Oh *dear*,' she repeated.

'You see what I mean,' Judd said gloomily. 'Even the sight of fish can bring Mr. Jefferson out in a rash if he's in one of his moods.' He shivered. 'And he's in one of them now, I'm afraid. You must prepare him something else.'

'I haven't got anything else.' Miranda rushed to the refrigerator. 'It's Friday. We never keep food here over the weekend.' Her eyes racked the shelves. 'An omelette is the only thing I can do.'

'That's better than nothing,' said Judd.

'An omelette prepared by a Madame Elise cook is considerably better than nothing,' Miranda said, unhappy to see the butler so distressed. 'Anyway, I'm sure Mr. Jefferson won't be annoyed when he realises what caused the misunderstanding. I take it he knows about Miss Robinson?'

'I whispered it in his ear when I suddenly realised he hadn't touched the prawns.' For the first time a faint smile brightened his features. 'You should have seen the look on his face when he saw those prawns. You'd have thought they were going to get up and bite him!'

Miranda laughed. 'It must be quite frightening to have such a bad allergy.' The butter in the pan was foaming and she tipped the egg mixture into it. It bubbled and she stirred it brusquely with a fork and then let it settle, moving the pan constantly and lowering the light as she did so. In a moment an omelette—golden brown outside and soft and creamy inside—lay on a warm plate and Judd carried it hurriedly into the dining room. What a shame Mr. Jefferson had had to return on a fish day, she thought, and what a pity that Bert had forgotten to mention the allergy. She had never heard of anyone being allergic to *all* kinds of fish and wondered if there was any hidden meaning behind the man's dislike of anything fishy. The idea made her smile, though she wiped it away as Bert ran in.

'Any potatoes going?'

'You know there aren't.'

'I know,' he confessed, 'but Mr. Jefferson sent me in anyhow. I don't think he finds the omelette substantial enough.'

Miranda threw up her hands and Bert went back to the dining room, not returning until the main course had been concluded and it was time to serve the sweet and cheese. Only when it came to the coffee did Miranda find time to sit down and pour a cup for herself. She had no appetite for lunch and her lack of hunger told her how nerve-racking she had found the last few hours. Still—Mr. Jefferson's allergy apart—she felt she had coped extremely well.

Judd thought so too and said it volubly when he returned to the kitchen, and, slipping off his jacket, sat down to rest. 'All the guests enjoyed the meal, Miss Jones,' he said, 'and two of them specifically sent their compliments to the cook.'

'I can do better than I did today,' Miranda said promptly.

'You have no cause to be making excuses. If there's any apologising to be done it should come from me. I really am sorry I forgot to warn you about Mr. Jefferson.'

'I'm sure it didn't kill him to have an omelette for lunch,' Miranda said bluffly, 'but I'd better check next week's menus. I understand he wasn't due back until the week after.'

'Dearie me, you're quite right. I'll find out from his secretary what days he'll be lunching in. Not that one can go by that. He's the sort of man who decides to be in or out at a moment's notice.'

'Now I know about his allergy I'll make sure there's always something on hand in the fridge. Chops or steak can be grilled without any problem.'

Bert came into the kitchen and interpreting his glance towards the oven, Miranda went over and drew out half a quiche. 'Aren't you going to join us?' Judd asked as she served them.

'Not today. I don't seem to have any appetite.'

'Not like Miss Robinson,' said Bert. 'She ate for two.'

'That's enough from you,' Judd warned, and Miranda smiled and began to put the rest of the dishes in the dishwasher.

'There's no need for you to do that,' the butler informed her. 'Mrs. Judd and Bert do it.'

Glad she was saved from doing this tedious chore, Miranda made sure all the electric equipment she had used was clean and that no food was left out of the refrigerator or larder. Then she went down the corridor to the cloakroom where she had left her outdoor clothes. She was halfway towards it when the door in front of her was flung open and a tall, dark-suited figure strode out, only stopping himself in time from colliding with her. Tilting back her head,

21

Miranda looked a long way up into a thin face marked by grey-green eyes and thick black brows whose colour was echoed by the equally dark hair slicked back from a high forehead. Murmuring an apology, she went to walk past, but he barred her way and once again her eyes travelled up the long lean length, noting the highly polished shoes, the narrow well-cut trousers and jacket and the startlingly white shirt.

'I presume you're the gnome in the kitchen?'

'I am the cook, yes,' she said in a prim voice.

His eyes took in the voluminous bunched-up apron and the ponytail kept in position by a rakishly-tied white swathe of material. 'The cook, eh? Well, you could have fooled me. Not that I'm in a position to judge your cooking after today's farce.'

'I beg your pardon?'

'You deserve to. That lunch today was a farce. I've frequently had to manage with an impromptu meal when I lunch in someone else's dining room, but I don't expect to do so when I'm in my own. An omelette,' he muttered darkly. 'Three thousand miles across the Atlantic and I'm met with an omelette!'

All at once she knew who he was, Blaize Howard Jefferson. What dreadful luck that she had to bump into him today! And if fate *had* wanted to play such a trick on her, couldn't it at least have waited until she had changed into her own clothes instead of being seen in this ridiculous get-up?

'I can't be blamed for what happened today, Mr. Jefferson.' Anger kept her voice cool. 'I wasn't aware of your allergy and——'

'When Miss Gould persuaded me to engage her company, it was on the strict understanding that there would be no mishaps of this kind. The premise on which she operates is that her clients are never faced with an emergency in their kitchen. If one cook walks out she undertakes to supply another without any resultant change in the rhythm.' His eyes raked her. 'In this instance I don't consider she's served me very well.'

'You can't blame Miss Gould for your allergy!'

'I can and I do. Today was the first emergency we've had, yet when it happens, her whole organisation breaks down.'

'An excellent luncheon was served to fourteen guests,' Miranda said icily. 'I fail to see how you can call that breaking down.'

'How would you describe *my* lunch?'

'As a creamy omelette cooked to perfection!'

There was no humour in his face as he glared at her. 'That was *not* what I meant, Miss—er——'

'Jones,' she said, and was suddenly a ghast at the way she had lost her temper. After all, she worked for Barbara—had considered it a golden opportunity in fact—and now here she was insulting a client. But in extricating herself she must be careful not to implicate Judd, even though he should rightly take the blame.

'Under normal circumstances, Mr. Jefferson,' she said in gentle tones, 'when Miss Gould replaces a cook the new one is always acquainted with the food likes and dislikes of her clients. This would have included your allergy, of course, but unfortunately Miss Robinson was taken ill before she could let us know this.'

'I know all that.' Mr. Jefferson was by no means appeased. 'But I would have thought that a cook employed by Miss Gould would have the intelligence to rustle up something better than an omelette.'

By dint of willpower Miranda controlled her temper. 'I've already explained to you, Mr. Jefferson, that today's circumstances were not normal. I can assure you such a mistake will not occur next week. If you're in to lunch when you're supposed to be out, there will always be chops or steak available for you.'

'And what happens when you actually *know* I'll be in? Will you make up special concoctions for me while the others are eating their Sole Florentine?'

'Of course I will. If fish is served, you'll always be offered something else.'

'I hope you live up to your word, Miss Jones.' He stepped back, signifying that the conversation was at an end.

Swiftly she went on her way and, in the seclusion of the cloakroom, found her hands were shaking so much that she could hardly undo her overall. What an insufferable, bad-tempered, supercilious man he was! And what bad luck that he should be the Managing Director. It took away all the joy of working here. How on earth had Mary Robinson managed to cope with such an irate boor? She must remember to ask Barbara if Mary had made any comments about him. Slipping into her skirt, she zipped it up and put on her blouse and jacket. Once again she looked petite and presentable, her dark hair a shining curtain round her face, her tilted eyes a darker aquamarine than usual because of her temper.

B. H. Jefferson. Without doubt those initials stood for Big Head. They were the two best words to describe him. With a snort, she went down the corridor to the lift.

CHAPTER TWO

'REALLY, Miranda,' Barbara said in exasperation. 'Did you have to argue with Mr. Jefferson the first time you meet him?'

'I wasn't the one to do the arguing. He happened to be in a flaming temper and he vented it on me. A normal man would have complimented me on the meal I turned out, not

24

acted as if I'd served up Cheddar cheese on burnt toast!'

'The poor thing was probably still hungry. You have to admit an omelette isn't a substantial lunch for a man. Particularly when he's flown in from the States.'

'He didn't flap his arms and fly *himself* over! He came on a jet—first class I've no doubt—and probably stuffed himself on caviar and champagne all the way!'

The aquamarine eyes flashed and Barbara said quickly: 'Not that I could have done any better than you. Especially when you were in the middle of serving a meal too. But I wouldn't have answered him back when he lost his temper.'

Miranda tried but failed to see Barbara remaining silent while she was harangued by a bad-tempered bully. However, to say so would be undiplomatic, and she shrugged in an acquiescent way, which immediately soothed her friend's irritation.

'It will make a good story to cheer Mary up when we go and see her,' Barbara smiled. 'I thought we could pop into the hospital tomorrow.'

'Fine,' said Miranda. 'If I have to cook at the bank for the next fortnight, I'll need all the counselling I can get.'

'I'm sure Mary has written down all her comments. That's one of the things I insist on all my cooks doing.'

'I'm sure she did. The only thing is I can't find the book.'

'It's in my handbag,' Mary Robinson said, when faced with the question the next afternoon. She was a buxom, fair-haired girl, paler than normal after her operation but already feeling well enough to sit up in bed and look with interest at the passing tea trays.

'I can't understand you having a set-to with Mr. Jefferson,' she continued. 'He's always been perfectly charming to me.'

Miranda thought it best not to go into further explanation. 'Does he have any other dislikes apart from being unable to eat fish?' she asked.

'None at all. In fact all the directors are easy to cater for, and Mr. Watson is an absolute poppet. He's the one responsible for the catering. The main thing to remember with Mr. Jefferson, though, is that he has a fetish about frozen vegetables. He likes everything to be fresh.'

This was not unreasonable and Miranda nodded. 'How long are you likely to be here?'

'Ten days. Then I'll go home for a week.' Mary winked at Barbara and then at Miranda. 'I'm not going to let you replace me at the bank permanently.'

'You needn't worry about that! When it does come my turn to do a stint in the kitchens, I'll make sure it isn't with the Lothian Bank!'

Miranda remembered this as she entered the gleaming kitchen on Monday morning, and tried to put all prejudice from her mind. Barbara and she had decided to divide the buying of provisions between them for the next week, after which another girl would be coming in to help out. But today they had started at five o'clock in order to finish shopping earlier than usual, and she was already so tired that she made herself a strong cup of coffee to revive her. She had spent part of the weekend going through the menus Mary had planned for this week, and had altered several of them to suit her own personal taste. She decided to re-check with Mr. Jefferson's secretary to find out when he was lunching in. She knew Judd normally did this, but was so anxious to prevent anything else going wrong that she knew she would not rest until she checked it herself.

Mr. Jefferson's secretary, Mrs. Linton, was an affable woman in early middle-age who did not seem at all in awe of her boss.

'He'll be in for lunch today, tomorrow and Friday,' she murmured, looking at the calf-skin diary on her desk. 'If he changes his mind about the other days I'll phone down to the kitchen myself and let you know.'

'That's awfully kind of you. After Friday, I don't want to fall foul of Big Head again.'

'Of who?' Mrs. Linton asked faintly.

'Big Head—those are his initials, aren't they? B.H.'

'Blaize Howard,' said the woman.

'Big Head suits him better,' said Miranda. 'How long have you been with him?'

'Ten years—I was the first secretary he had at the bank.'

'Don't tell me he's been Managing Director since then?'

'Good heavens no! He was only twenty-two. He became M.D. when he was thirty. The youngest ever to be appointed.'

'Ability or inheritance?' Miranda asked sarcastically.

'Both,' said an equally sarcastic voice behind her, and Mrs. Linton's startled expression told Miranda the identity of the intruder.

The Fates are not only laughing at me, Miranda decided, they're positively having hysterics. Trying to look unconcerned, she faced Blaize Howard Jefferson, immaculate as ever in the inevitable dark suit and white shirt. He seemed taller than she remembered, and she was glad she had not yet slipped into her flat-heeled working shoes but was wearing high-heeled ones. They not only emphasised her shapely legs but added a further inch to her five foot two. Despite this, the top of her head barely reached his chin.

'When you're ready, Mrs. Linton,' he said, ignoring Miranda, 'I have some letters to give you.'

'I'll be with you right away, Mr. Jefferson.' The woman stood up, notebook in hand, and crossed the room to his side. He stepped back to let her precede him into his office and as she did, he glanced directly at Miranda.

'If the bank cook wishes to know the whereabouts of any of our directors, Miss Jones, she should ask Judd or Mr. Watson. I do not expect her to waste the time of my personal secretary.'

It was a justifiable criticism and Miranda was sorry to have merited it, but it was too late to do anything other than apologise, which she did as charmingly as she could, hating herself for every grovelling word. 'I only checked with Mrs. Linton because I want everything to run smoothly from now on, Mr. Jefferson.'

'So do I,' he said coldly.

Head high, she marched to the door and was halfway through it when he called her name.

Hand on the knob, she turned. 'Yes?'

'Despite what you think to the contrary, Miss Jones, I take a normal size in hats.'

It was several seconds before she understood what he meant, then colour flamed into her face, darkening further as she saw the malevolent grin on his own before she slammed the door behind her and raced up to the top floor. He was not just a bad-tempered tyrant, he was a sarcastic bully too!

Anger put Miranda on her mettle and the meal she presented that day was faultless. But if she expected any praise from Mr. Jefferson, she waited in vain, though Judd did say that a couple of directors had asked if there was a new cook in the kitchen.

'I told them we had an Amazon,' he said, and grinned broadly at her. 'And if capability went with size, so you would be.'

It was a pretty turn of compliment and she chuckled, her tiredness ebbing slightly, though it returned again as she left the bank and walked towards the subway. Barbara had taken the van and she found it a solitary experience to strap-hang in a swaying train, crowded even though it was not yet the rush hour.

She said nothing to Barbara of her second unhappy encounter with the Managing Director of the Lothian Bank.

28

Just remembering the incident made her squirm. One day her tongue would get her into such serious trouble that not even her femininity and looks would get her out of it.

Tuesday morning was more of a rush than Monday, for she was delayed at the market and did not arrive at the bank until ten-thirty. There were two dining rooms to cater for today: the main one where there were twelve for lunch, and the smaller room where two directors were dining with four guests, one of whom was a vegetarian and the other a diabetic. This meant preparing a different hors d'oeuvres for the vegetarian and a special sweet for the diabetic. However, there were no specific orders to follow for the main dining room and she set about preparing this first, having already half cooked the entrée the day before. It was a specially cured gammon bought from a private source of Barbara's which she guarded zealously, and chewing a snippet as she covered the rest with honey and mustard, Miranda appreciated why, for it was the tastiest she had eaten. It inspired her to greater culinary efforts and she scrapped her original intention of puréed potatoes and buttered peas to make little individual spinach soufflés and gratins dauphinoises—potatoes sliced finely on a mandolin, covered with cream and baked in a slow oven to be grated with cheese in the last half hour. Even the sweet surpassed itself, and meringues glistened white as snow atop a rich chocolate mousse delicately flavoured with rum and hiding succulent slices of skinned mandarins.

'There's a lot of money around today,' Bert commented at lunch time when he popped into the kitchen to substitute a used napkin for a clean one. 'Oil sheiks, I think they are. Wearing their bed sheets and funny headgear.'

'It's called a burnous,' Miranda explained. 'You shouldn't make fun of the different way other people dress. Our clothes probably look just as peculiar to them.' Bert looked as though he found this hard to believe and went out

29

whistling cheerily, though when he returned some half hour later he looked so glum that Miranda asked him what was wrong.

'I'm not sure,' he said, 'but Mr. Jefferson looks like a dam fit to burst.'

'You mean he's in a temper about something?'

'He must be. He's smiling all over his face and very la-de-dah, which is always a sign that he's getting ready to explode.'

'Well, he isn't going to explode in here,' Miranda said with conviction. Not even Big Head Jefferson could fault today's lunch, and the one in the small dining room had already come in for lavish praise. 'It can't be anything that *we* did wrong,' Miranda asserted.

'Not we,' said Bert. 'Judd. I'm afraid he slipped up again. It's because of his missus. He's so worried about her that he hasn't got a mind to anything else.'

'I didn't know she was ill,' said Miranda.

'Some sort of depression,' Bert confided. 'He keeps it a secret in case Mr. Jefferson fires him. I mean, they live on the premises and he wouldn't like to think there was a loony wandering around.'

'A person who's depressed is not a loony,' Miranda corrected. 'Lots of people get depression. Even the wonderful Mr. Jefferson should know that. Anyway,' she said anxiously, 'what exactly did Judd forget to do?'

Bert was on the point of telling her when the bell from the dining room summoned him back, and Miranda was left to place the sweet on the trolley, ready for Judd to serve. What on earth could have gone wrong this time? Try as she would she could not see where a mistake had been made and when the plates from the main course were returned to the kitchen she stared in puzzlement at the pink slices of gammon left untouched on several of them. Picking up a knife, she carved a piece from the joint and tried it, wondering if something had gone wrong with it in the last few moments in the oven. But no, it was as tasty as when she had first tried it. She had just set down the knife when a quick step on the tiled floor brought Blaize Jefferson into the kitchen. His arrival was so unexpected that she stood silent—not that she would have had much opportunity to speak if she had wanted to, for at the sight of her, the rage he had been keeping in check erupted and, without raising his voice, a tidal wave of fury engulfed her.

'Of all the addle-pated, incompetent muddleheads it's ever been my misfortune to encounter, *you are the worst*! If Miss Gould can't find anyone other than you to replace Miss Robinson, then you can tell her from me that I'm tearing up the contract. Do I make myself clear?'

Horrified, she went on staring at him.

'Well?' he barked. 'What's happened to your tongue? Cooked it with the gammon?'

'Don't be so rude!' she flared.

'I'm surprised you have the intelligence to know I'm being rude. But obviously what passes for a brain in your head hasn't yet put you wise to the way you've insulted my guests.'

'How can I insult your guests when I've never met them?'

'By serving them ham,' he retorted.

'They're Arabs,' she cried, 'not Jews.'

'Heaven spare me!' He spoke between clenched teeth. 'Don't you know that Mohammedans don't eat pork either? And even if you *were* ignorant, I know Judd told you they were coming, because I reminded him of it myself yesterday and he said he would tell you.'

Miranda was about to say that Judd had told her no such thing when she remembered what Bert had said to her earlier. She closed her mouth and remained mute, realising that to defend herself would bring Blaize Jefferson's wrath

31

down on Judd at a time when the old man had enough personal misery to cope with.

'I assume your silence to be one of apology and not dumb insolence?' Blaize Jefferson said icily.

'I'm certainly sorry if your guests thought I was insulting them,' she whispered, 'and if it will be of any use I'm prepared to apologise to them personally. But one thing I will not do is to stand here and have *you* insulting *me*. You're the rudest, most bad-mannered boor I've ever met! Worse than that, you're also unfair.'

'Unfair?' he echoed.

'For accusing a person without hearing what they have to say first. Your name shouldn't be Jefferson—it should be Jeffreys. Judge Jeffreys! And I'm sure you know what *he* did!'

'The hanging judge,' he said curtly. 'But I haven't hanged you, Miss Jones. I've merely fired you and you can count yourself lucky.'

'I'm lucky I don't have to see you again! And you can get Bert to prepare your beastly coffee—I won't.' To signify her liberation she whipped off her apron. Only as she did so did she remember she wasn't wearing a dress and with a gasp of horror she held the apron in front of her. 'Get out of my kitchen!' she stormed.

'*My* kitchen,' he reminded her, 'and you're the one who's leaving! But put on a dress before you go. You're working at a bank, not a striptease club!'

Scarlet with rage and embarrassment, Miranda rushed out in a whirl of blue satin petticoat. In the cloakroom she splashed cold water on her burning face and then put on her dress. It would have been easy to defend herself had she wished to implicate Judd, but even now she did not regret keeping quiet.

Tightening the belt round her small waist, she opened the door, looked out quickly to make sure the corridor was deserted and then sped towards the lift. Going down to the ground floor she began to envisage the scene that must have taken place in the dining room when the ham had been served to the three sheiks. No wonder Mr. Jefferson had been sitting at the table looking fit to burst. If she were still not so angry she could have laughed. But the fury engendered by Blaize Jefferson's sarcasm had not yet died, though she knew that by the time she recounted the scene to Barbara she would be able to turn it into a funny story. Of course, the funniest part was when she had whipped off her apron and stood in front of him in a wisp of satin. But at the moment even this failed to bring a smile to her face and, as the lift reached the ground floor, she marched across the banking hall. It was ornately furnished: the floor carpeted, the desks teak and the clerks all carbon copies of their Managing Director. Several of them eyed her with interest as she went past them to the main front door.

'I have a message for you, Miss Jones,' the commissionaire said as she reached him. 'You're wanted back upstairs.'

Miranda hesitated, tempted to walk past him and out of the building. As if he suspected this was her intention, the man stepped in front of her.

'Mr. Jefferson wants to see you,' he said. 'He just this moment telephoned down. He's in his office.'

Muttering below her breath, Miranda turned and went back the way she had come. If he dared to be rude to her again she would hit him! Regardless of the consequences she would slap him across the face. Eyes blazing like blue fires, she entered Mrs. Linton's office and received a welcoming smile.

'So we *did* catch you in time, Miss Jones. Mr. Jefferson will be so pleased.'

Since Mr. Jefferson had recently and clearly indicated that his pleasure would be *never* to see her again, Miranda wondered whether he had gone out of his head. Nonetheless she followed his secretary across the carpeted floor and into the hall of halls.

Like a sleek black panther Blaize Jefferson sat in a black leather armchair behind an ebony desk. The carpet underfoot was charcoal grey, the walls and drapes silver grey and the paintings modern and magnificent. A Braque, a Klee and a Hockney were the three she managed to glimpse before the man stood up and motioned her to sit in front of him.

'Why do you want to see me?' she asked truculently, refusing his offer of a chair.

Because she had not sat down he remained standing too. 'I want to apologise—though actually you don't deserve it, since you're to blame for not telling me that Judd forgot to inform you that three of our guests were sheiks.'

She flashed him a look from beneath her lashes, but not so quick that he did not see it.

'Yes,' he went on, 'Judd told me that he was at fault.'

'And from what gallows is he hanging now?' she asked sarcastically.

Deliberately the man looked at his watch. 'By now he should be halfway to Harley Street with his wife. I've arranged for her to see my own doctor. If people will persist in hiding facts from me, they should at least have the courtesy not to blame me when I don't do anything to help them.'

'Judd didn't blame you. He was just too scared to tell you about his wife in case——' She stopped, angry for having broken a confidence.

'Don't worry, Miss Jones,' a well-manicured hand pointed to a chair. 'Do sit down. *I* am tired even if you aren't.'

She complied, keeping to the edge of the seat to make sure her feet still touched the carpet. People in the City

34

were like giants and assumed everyone else was the same.

'You look as uncomfortable as I feel,' he said unexpectedly.

'You deserve to feel uncomfortable!'

'That isn't a very ladylike thing to say.'

'I don't feel very ladylike towards you.'

He eyed her stonily. So must he look at a bankrupt client who was demanding money from him, she thought, and turned her profile to him: a small nose slightly tip-tilted, her mouth sweetly curved and full but her soft rounded chin set firm with determination. 'I accept your apology, Mr. Jefferson, but please may I leave now? Otherwise I'll get caught in the rush hour and have to strap-hang home.'

'I shouldn't have thought you were big enough to reach a strap! Sorry,' he said quickly as she glared at him, 'I didn't mean to be rude.' He coughed slightly. 'I hope you'll forget the—er—the little contretemps we had earlier and continue to remain here as Miss—er—as the other young lady's replacement. Apart from the mishap with the sheiks, the luncheon was excellent, and I'm sure that once Judd's mind is at rest about his wife, he won't forget to relay any necessary messages to you.' He clasped his hands together on the blotter in front of him, the long fingers intertwining one with the other. 'Please forgive me, Miss Jones, I really am most abject.' He accompanied the words with a wide smile that completely transformed his face.

Miranda was astonished by it. When austere and aloof, he had also been exceptionally handsome, but now that he was smiling, he was devastating. His eyes crinkled at the corners, his mouth softened and curved back to show brilliant white teeth and he looked years younger. 'He's a dish,' Miranda thought. 'A delectable dish.'

'Can I take it you'll forgive me?' he said.

'Yes, Mr. Jefferson.'

'Good.' As though he had done his duty he stood up at

once and went to the door, holding out his hand to her as he reached it. 'Good afternoon, Miss Jones, and thank you for being so magnanimous.'

She was out of the room and on the other side of the door before she had a chance to say anything else, and only the creak of Mrs. Linton's chair brought her back to an awareness of her present surroundings.

'Not so bad, is he, when you get to know him?' his secretary smiled.

'No,' Miranda said primly, 'he isn't.' Feeling as though the carpet beneath her feet had turned into a cloud, she walked out.

CHAPTER THREE

To Miranda's disappointment she saw nothing of Blaize Jefferson for the rest of that week. But she heard a great deal about him from Mr. Judd, who was now her firm friend, believing it was her remarks to Mr. Jefferson which had resulted in his taking an active interest in Mrs. Judd's health.

'It had nothing to do with me,' Miranda protested for the umpteenth time on the Friday afternoon as she was preparing to leave. 'You were the one who told Mr. Jefferson your wife was ill!'

'I would never have mentioned my private affairs if Mr. Jefferson hadn't fired you, so in a way you *are* responsible.'

Since the butler seemed determined to turn her into his angel she decided it was wiser to accept the position. 'How is your wife getting on?' she asked.

'It's too early to say for sure, but there has definitely been an improvement. The specialist warned me it would take a couple of weeks at least before we saw any great difference in her, but just knowing her condition is curable has taken a weight off my mind. Which reminds me—if you'll forgive the pun—that Mr. Watson said he's coming to see you. He's in charge of the catering, you know, and would have been in to see you before except that he was in America with Mr. Jefferson and only came back yesterday.'

'What's he like?' Miranda asked.

'A nice young gentleman.'

The reply told Miranda nothing, but she considered it unwise to show too much curiosity. 'I'm glad I have the weekend ahead of me,' she confided. 'I feel absolutely exhausted.'

'You work hard, a little thing like you.'

As always when her size was mentioned, Miranda bristled. 'I'm as strong as an ox!'

'You still look as if a puff of wind would blow you away.'

Miranda smiled and stretched her legs out in front of her, shapely legs, as was the rest of her figure, which was shown to advantage in the cool uncluttered lines of her white uniform dress. With her heart-shaped face and swinging black hair she looked like a modern version of Florence Nightingale and could as easily have been envisaged carrying a lamp along a dark ward as an egg beater in a kitchen.

Coming into the room unheard and unseen, Alan Watson found her an enchanting spectacle, and had he been the sort of man to believe in love at first sight, would have said that this had happened to him, but because he was a cautious young man, he came to the conclusion that it was merely the shock of seeing someone so unusually lovely and fragile sitting in a straight-backed wooden chair in the large, clinical-looking kitchen. Had this enchanting little thing concocted that superb luncheon today? The surprise was evident on his face as he came forward, hand outstretched.

'Miss Jones. I'm Alan Watson. I gather you've been coping magnificently during Miss Robinson's illness.'

Flushing, Miranda jumped up and they shook hands.

'How long will Miss Robinson be in the hospital?' he continued. 'The directors would like to send her some flowers and books.'

'She'll be in hospital another week and then she's going home to recuperate. She had complications and the doctor thinks she should take things easy for a month.'

'Good advice.' Alan Watson smiled and Miranda responded to it. He was about the same age as his Managing Director but nowhere near as good-looking, for, with eyes that were bemused by hazel ones and hair as black as her own, she was unimpressed by brown eyes and fair waves, though she did acknowledge that he was tall and broad and looked as though he would be fun to know.

'Have you finished here?' he was asking.

'Yes. I'll be leaving in a few moments. Did you want to talk to me?'

Alan Watson nodded. 'Most of the directors will be away for a week at the end of this month, and we'll be closing the kitchen for that time too.'

'I didn't realise a bank ever closed,' she said.

'We'll still be open for business,' he said, 'but Mr. Jefferson doesn't think it worthwhile to keep the kitchen going just for a handful of us.'

'It seems a strange economy.'

'It isn't a question of economy, Miss Jones. Judd and his wife will be away too, and it would mean getting in a temporary butler. If we stick to coffee and biscuits with the odd cheese sandwich, Bert can manage on his own. You'll be paid in the normal way, of course,' he added quickly.

'I wasn't thinking about that,' Miranda said candidly. 'Merely that I would have thought it more convenient to have had me here. I'm quite willing to come in, and if you're going to pay me anyway, I might as well do so. I needn't prepare elaborate meals, but at least I would see you had something better than bread and cheese.'

'I'll have a word with B.H. and let you know.' Alan Watson moved away and then hesitated. 'I'm driving into town so I can give you a lift. Does the vicinity of Claridge's suit you?'

'Very much. I'm going window-shopping in Bond Street.'

'Then I'll meet you downstairs in fifteen minutes.'

Watching him go, Miranda wished the offer had come from Blaize Jefferson. It was annoying to think that three days had gone by without her even catching a glimpse of him, and more annoying to feel convinced that the man himself had not given her a single thought. He had probably even forgotten she worked here. Preparing the lunch on Wednesday and Thursday she had been conscious only of the fact that he was not in the dining room, and today, knowing he was, she had taken pains to present a superb meal, hoping it might encourage him to send in a word of appreciation. But there had been nothing.

Cross with herself for thinking of him, she changed into her outdoor clothes and went downstairs at the appointed time. A moment later Alan Watson appeared, gloves and umbrella in hand, looking so much like a City gent that Miranda had to restrain a giggle. He led her down to the lower ground floor where there was garage space for half a dozen cars.

'The élite of the Lothian Bank,' he grinned, waving his arm at the gleaming cars. 'All the others have to fight for space in the National Car Park.'

She stared with interest at two opulent foreign cars, a sedate Rover and a vast silver-grey Rolls that almost hid a tiny black Mini Cooper. 'Mr. Jefferson's?' she said, pointing to the Rolls.

'Mr. Jefferson's,' Alan Watson replied, pointing to the Mini.

She was so surprised that she could not hide it and he gave her another grin as he opened the door of the Rover for her. 'B.H. has a Rolls,' he admitted, 'but he never uses it when he's driving himself. He's a maniac in a Mini, though, goes up the motorway like a bomb.'

She could well imagine it. He was probably a road hog too, but she refrained from saying so and sedately took her seat. They left the garage and headed towards the West End.

Alan Watson was easy to talk to and before Miranda realised it she had told him a great deal about herself and her background. She learned very little of his beyond the fact that he had been a director of the bank for two years, and had known its Managing Director from their Oxford days.

'He was one of the few men there to get a Double Blue—cricket and rowing,' he explained.

'What about academically?' she asked.

'A Triple First in Economics. He was all set for politics when this job cropped up.'

'You mean to be M.D.?'

'Lord no!' the man chuckled. 'But the chance to become one of the Lothian Bank's young men. He didn't remain one of them for very long. He soon became *the* one.'

'Did you join the bank at the same time?' she asked.

'I joined a rival one, but once B.H. was in power he brought me in.'

'Are you personal friends as well?'

He nodded, but to Miranda's disgust offered no further information. She would have liked to know more of Blaize Jefferson's private life, but aware that her curiosity would not go unnoticed, she held her tongue. They reached Claridge's Hotel and the car came to a stop.

'I'll be seeing you around,' he said as she jumped out. 'Enjoy your window-gazing!'

Smiling her thanks, she set off towards Bond Street, conscious of him watching her as she went. She knew he had found her attractive, but his admiration meant nothing to her, and as she turned the corner into the main thoroughfare she forgot him completely. Her main concern was that in ten days' time the bank kitchen would close for a week and by the time it reopened, Mary would have returned. Ruefully she acknowledged that once she left the bank she would never see its Managing Director again. They lived in different worlds and it was only by luck that she had even got to know him, if one could so describe their stormy encounters. Her arched eyebrows drew together. It was crazy and illogical to keep thinking of him. He was not the first good-looking man she had met, though he was the first one on whom she had made no impact. She was far more used to men reacting to her the way Alan Watson had done—with immediate interest and admiration—but as far as Blaize Jefferson was concerned she could have looked like the back of a bus. Probably if she had, he might have been more courteous towards her, the way she gathered that he was towards Mrs. Judd.

Slowing her pace, she concentrated on a display of summer dresses, but in each one that she imagined herself she also imagined a tall, black-haired escort. It was chemical attraction, nothing more, plus the fact that it was late spring and the time when a young man's fancy was supposed to turn to thoughts of love and the woman's turned to ways and means of making sure his thoughts remained there. She tried to picture the kind of girl whom Blaize Jefferson might find attractive and wondered dejectedly whether he was already married. But no, that wasn't the case, for the one nugget of information she had gleaned in this past week was that he was still single. Of course that didn't mean he was unattached. She pushed open the door of the dress shop and walked in. Her confidence was at a low ebb and a couple of summer dresses would do wonders for her jaded spirit.

Returning to the bank on Monday morning Miranda felt a sense of homecoming. She was used to the kitchen and could prepare things with far more confidence than she had in her first week. She could even think of its Managing Director with detachment, having decided in the last two days that her interest in him was caused more by pique at his disinterest in her than by a genuine liking. After all, he was not even her type. Her boy-friends had always been affable and easy-going, amused by her frankness and charmed by her vivacious beauty, unlike Mr. Jefferson who, apart from his brief apology for having fired her, had always been rude and sarcastic.

Judd handed her an amended guest list and she saw that the initials of B.H.J. were set down for every day of the week. There would also be two dining rooms to cook for on Wednesday and Thursday, which necessitated bringing in outside help. Miranda was glad that the extra girl Barbara had found had now taken over the buying of provisions, for it meant she no longer had to get up at an ungodly hour and instead could have a leisurely breakfast before coming here.

Contentedly she set to work, checking the store cupboard to make sure she had everything she required and making notes of food that needed replenishing. Apart from preparing lunch she was responsible for the cakes and biscuits served at mid-morning and tea time, and having learnt from Judd that B.H. had a sweet tooth, she concentrated on preparing the most delicious cakes she could.

At eleven o'clock the fragrant smell of warm yeast dough filled the kitchen. The Danish pastries she was making would be too hot to serve this morning but would be delicious at four o'clock. She tested the rising dough with her fingers, then set to work to roll it out into little crescents and balls stuffed with cinnamon, sugar and raisins. When

42

this was done it was time to put the finishing touches to the lunch and she worked without cessation until the first silver platter of canapés was carried into the dining room.

Monday set the pattern for the rest of the week, which was an extremely hard-working one for her. There was so much to prepare that she frequently stayed late, leaving the refrigerator full of half-cooked dishes ready for the next day. Thursday was the most tiring day of all, particularly as it came after Wednesday's large luncheon party, and Miranda felt she had been working non-stop—as indeed she had—for she had not finished her preparation until five o'clock the day before and had begun at nine this morning. But the appreciation of the guests—as recounted by Judd and Bert—was ample compensation, as were the empty dishes that rolled back into the kitchen.

'You really did them proud today,' said Bert, rolling his eyes. 'I've never seen B.H. looking so pleased with himself. You'd have thought he'd done the cooking rather than you.'

'He cooks up the business deals,' Judd said.

'Highly spiced some of them are, too,' Bert retorted. 'The *Sunday Gazette* had a real go at him last week.'

'The more successful a man is the more his critics carp.' Judd's frown indicated that the conversation was at an end and Bert moved off with the coffee tray. 'Young people these days have no respect for their betters,' Judd muttered, setting peppermint creams on two silver dishes.

'Because a person is rich it doesn't make them better,' Miranda could not help saying, 'and one shouldn't be proud just because one is clever or lucky in business.'

'Mr. Jefferson is clever, not lucky,' the butler reproved. 'He's worked extremely hard for his success. That's what people tend to overlook—all the hard work that goes on behind the scenes.'

'You can say that again,' said Miranda, and looked around at the pots and pans that were waiting to be cleaned, a job which, today, she could thankfully leave to the additional kitchen help.

'You've really done the dining room proud today,' Judd said kindly. 'Why don't you go off now? I'll see about serving the lunch for the kitchen staff.'

'I'll be fine when I get my second wind,' Miranda smiled, 'but thanks for the offer.' Afraid to sit down, lest she feel too tired to get up again, she bustled about laying the table, though she herself was too exhausted to have any appetite and would be content with coffee. It was as she was sipping this that the internal telephone rang and Bert, nearest to it, took the message.

'That was Mrs. Linton,' he said. 'Big Brother wants to see you.'

'To thank you personally, I'm sure,' smiled Judd. 'He had two portions of the sweet and whispered to me that he'd like another one with his tea.'

Miranda grew warm with pleasure. She had been waiting for such a call the entire week. She longed to rush into the cloakroom and put on her dress, but knew that to do so would look as if she were trying too hard. Deliberately she contented herself with combing her hair smooth—it always seemed to stand on end when she was cooking—applied a dusting of powder to her flushed cheeks and sped downstairs into Blaize Jefferson's office.

'He isn't here,' Mrs. Linton said as she walked in. 'You'll find him in the Directors' Room.'

Miranda hid her disappointment, for this meant she would not be seeing him alone. In the past week she had learned a fair amount about the way the bank was run. The Managing Director was the only one who had a private office; all the other directors worked from a very large room, each with their own desk and telephone, though their individual secretaries had their own office. It had seemed an odd arrangement until Bert—who was her main inform-

44

ant—told her Mr. Jefferson preferred it this way, for it meant that the directors always knew what was going on and less time was spent in acquainting each other with what was being done.

'I think his real reason is that he likes to see where the knives are kept,' he had added darkly, a comment which Miranda knew to be unjustified, since the other thing she had learned was that Blaize Jefferson was held in great respect by everyone who worked for him.

'Where is the Directors' Room?' she asked aloud.

'On the left at the end of the corridor,' Mrs. Linton said, and Miranda found herself in a large rectangular room, furnished with fine weaves and leather and the usual highly expensive *objets d'art*. Merchant banks, it seemed, vied with each other to achieve a reputation as connoisseurs, and the Lothian, more than most, had a reputation for avantgarde works.

Blaize Jefferson was seated at a desk in front of the large window that overlooked Moorgate, and Miranda was glad that the two desks closest to him were unoccupied. At least their conversation would not be overheard. The occupants of the other four desks smiled at her in a friendly fashion as she went towards the window.

'Good afternoon, Miss Jones.' Blaize Jefferson was also smiling as he indicated to her to sit down. She was glad to obey, for she was trembling in a most foolish way. It was more than a week since she had seen him and it was all she could do not to stare at him. Instead she kept her eyes on the wall that rose behind one broad navy mohair-covered shoulder. The shirt was white—as she knew it would be—and the tie dark and conservative. But the pale face was friendly, the hazel eyes more green than grey and looking at her with obvious warmth. Quickly she re-focused on the wall.

'You wanted to see me, Mr. Jefferson?'

'To thank you for the splendid lunch you prepared today and the splendid lunches you've put on for the entire week. I'm sorry we had two big parties in succession, but I believe Mr. Watson instructed Judd to see you had all the help you required?'

'Yes, thank you, everyone has been most kind.' She longed to say more but resolutely compressed her lips.

'Do relax,' he said quietly, and reaching out for a beautiful enamel box, offered her a cigarette.

'I don't smoke,' she said, 'but I would love a piece of chocolate.'

'I beg your pardon?' He looked astonished and then quickly recovered himself. 'I'm afraid I don't have any chocolate.' He opened a drawer and peered into it doubtfully. 'I can ask Mrs. Linton. I believe she has peppermints.'

'No, thank you.' Miranda's cheeks flamed and she could have kicked herself. But nervousness always made her talk too much and just having him lean towards her with a cigarette box had been her undoing. "I'm mad," she thought wildly. "I've never reacted to a man like this before. What's the matter with me? There's nothing so wonderful about him." To prove it she deliberately took her eyes from the wall and stared at him. He was still looking into the drawer, giving her a view of his rather severe profile. His brow was high and unlined, the nose slightly long but straight and the mouth relaxed and quirking slightly at the corners as though he were trying not to laugh.

'As you've got such a sweet tooth yourself,' she blurted out, 'I thought your drawer would have been full of chocolates!'

'It's *because* I have a sweet tooth that I do *not* keep a drawer full of chocolates,' he said, and closed it with a slight bang. 'You're out of luck, Miss Jones, it's either peppermints or nothing.'

'Nothing,' she said and, because she dearly wanted to go on talking to him, stood up in an effort to prove that she didn't.

'Where are you going, Miss Jones?'

'I thought you'd finished with me.'

'I've finished thanking you, but I haven't finished speaking.'

'I'm sorry,' she mumbled, and sat down again. 'Miss Robinson should be back by the time you re-open after the holiday. She wanted to come back next week, but the doctor——'

'Please,' a long-fingered hand was held up and Miranda subsided. 'Do you always talk so much?'

'Only when I'm nervous,' she said truthfully.

'You're surely not nervous of me?'

'I'm petrified!'

His mouth twitched. 'I don't bite, you know.'

'You've given every indication of wanting to do so.'

His lips clamped tight. 'We got off on the wrong foot, Miss Jones,' he said abruptly. 'I've already apologised for that.'

'I wasn't referring to it again,' she said quickly. 'Merely trying to explain why you—why I've been talking so much.'

'Well, you can relax now, content in the knowledge that I consider you highly efficient and an excellent replacement for Miss Robinson. In fact we would all be delighted to have you stay with us permanently.'

'I couldn't do that, I'm afraid,' she said.

'I thought not,' he said, far too promptly to please her. 'Though perhaps you may be able to help me in another way.' He picked up a thin gold pencil and twirled it between his fingers. Miranda watched the nervous gesture with fascination, wondering what he had to say that was making him hesitant.

'I'm not sure whether I shouldn't have spoken to Miss

Gould first,' he continued, 'but then I thought that as you were here it would be as well to check with you before I did so. I mean, if you weren't agreeable there would be no point in my taking it further.'

Having no idea what he was talking about, she stared into his face, her slanting eyes wide and ingenous.

'My own cook wishes to take a week off,' he explained, 'but she won't do so if I can't make other arrangements. I was wondering if you would be able to help me. Of course it would mean you having to live in the country. My house is in Sussex.'

Miranda swallowed hard. He was asking her to be a temporary cook at his home. It was a request she had never expected and so different from the one she had hoped he would make—she had stupidly seen him inviting her to have dinner with him as recompense for her hard work this week—that she was lost for words.

'Of course, if you don't want to do it, I quite understand,' he said. 'Perhaps one of the other young women Miss Gould employs. . . .'

This was adding insult to injury and Miranda's head tilted sharply. So if he couldn't have her he would be quite happy with one of Barbara's other girls, would he? The temptation to tell him what he could do with his precious job was very strong, but she held it back. After all, just because the offer was different from what she had hoped for, it did not mean she should look a gift horse in the mouth. And a gift horse it certainly was. Working at his home she would at least have the opportunity of seeing him on a more personal level than if she remained here. Anyway, she wouldn't be remaining here, so working for him in ·the country for a week was the next best thing. If she could not get him to look at her with some degree of interest during that time, she would eat the two cotton dresses she had bought the other day.

'I'm sure Miss Gould would be happy to arrange for me to help you, Mr. Jefferson.' She was delighted at how cool she sounded. 'When exactly will it be?'

'In a fortnight's time. We'll pay you the same amount of money and——'

'Please arrange that with Miss Gould,' she said quickly.

'Very well.' He set down his pencil. 'Is there anything you would like to know about the job?'

'Where do you live?' she asked.

'On the Sussex Downs, fifteen minutes' run from Shoreham.'

'Who will I have to cook for apart from yourself?'

'The weekend guests and the staff. It's a fairly big house and I do a lot of entertaining. But I'll limit it for the week you're with me.'

'You needn't do that,' she assured him. 'I enjoy cooking.'

'That's quite evident. If you didn't you would never be able to turn out such excellent meals. That gateau you served today was excellent.'

'I'll make it for you at home.'

'You must,' he said. 'And perhaps you could give the recipe to my own cook.'

Instantly her joy evaporated. How quickly he was already putting her out of his life! She stood up. 'Will that be all, Mr. Jefferson?'

He nodded and rose with her. 'You won't be in the week after next, of course, as the kitchen is closed, so I suggest you come to Sussex on the Friday rather than the Monday, then Mrs. Holden can go off a few days earlier.'

'Will you be entertaining that weekend?' Miranda asked.

'There'll possibly be a few guests,' he replied, 'but you needn't worry about the food. I'll see Mrs. Holden stocks up with everything you require, and there's a car and chauffeur at your disposal if you should need to go into Brighton.'

His tone, rather than his words, told her he was already thinking of other things, and murmuring goodbye Miranda left the room, disconsolately aware that he had resumed his seat and was busy looking at papers even before she had closed the door behind her.

Back in the cloakroom she stared at herself, gaining no joy from what she saw. As far as Blaize Jefferson was concerned she could have looked like Dracula's wife. Tears of annoyance made her eyes sparkle like jewels and she blinked them away angrily.

'You fool!' she said to herself, knowing miserably that his disinterest in her had in no way affected her interest in *him*.

CHAPTER FOUR

MIRANDA did not see Blaize Jefferson the following week, nor did he contact her, leaving it to Barbara to tell her she had received a letter from Mrs. Linton confirming that Miranda would be working personally for him for ten days. To restore some confidence in herself Miranda indulged in an orgy of shopping and social life. She was not short of boy-friends and she went out with a different one every night, finally drawing comment from Barbara, who suggested it might be a good idea if she stayed at home for a couple of evenings.

'I've never known you so determinedly gay,' she commented. 'What's wrong, Miranda? Running away from something?'

'Don't be silly. What should I be running away from?'

'A man. That's the usual reason.'

'There's no special man in my life,' Miranda said firmly. 'I just felt I was getting into a rut and I wanted to have a good time. Anyway, I'll be stuck in the country for a week, so I'll have bags of opportunity to catch up on my sleep.'

'You didn't need to accept Mr. Jefferson's offer.' Barbara looked anxious. 'I thought I'd made that quite clear.'

'I'm looking forward to going,' Miranda insisted. 'I'm not complaining.'

'What's he like? You've hardly spoken about him since you told me he apologised to you.'

'There's been nothing more to tell. I never see him.'

'He's young, isn't he? Mary said he was a dish.'

'We don't all like the same food,' said Miranda dryly.

'That's true,' Barbara chuckled. 'The last man Mary described that way was five foot three and bald. She fell for his smile,' Barbara added, 'and she never noticed the rest of him!'

Miranda knew the feeling only too well, for her liking for Blaize was just as illogical; only in her case she had fallen for outward appearances; the inner man—were she ever to know him—was probably wholly disagreeable.

The following day was her last one at the Bank and she was touched when Bert and Judd presented her with a bunch of flowers and seemed genuinely sad to see her go.

'I'll pop in and see you,' she promised, 'and once Mary is back you'll forget me.'

'We might forget *you*,' Bert replied, 'but not your hazelnut gateau!'

Miranda laughed and promised to make one especially for him.

'Don't forget,' he said, 'or I'll come and haunt you.'

It was a chastening prospect and she was still smiling at it as she left the bank. She paused on the pavement, waiting for a lull in the traffic before crossing the road, and a car glided slowly in her direction and stopped abreast of her.

'Hi,' said Alan Watson. 'Climb aboard and I'll give you a lift.'

'You don't know where I'm going.'

'No matter. I'll take you there anyway.'

Gratefully she took her place in the car and gave a sigh of pleasure as she sank back on the soft seat.

'After all the cooking you've been doing in the past few weeks,' he said, 'you must be exhausted.'

'That hasn't tired me, but I didn't get to bed until three o'clock this morning.' She wriggled her toes. 'My escort thought my feet were nicer to stand on than the floor!'

He chuckled. 'I'm glad to see you lead an active social life. I was half afraid you were tied to the kitchen.'

She said nothing and they drove for a few moments in silence. It gave her an opportunity to take a good look at him and she saw he was nicer than she had first thought, if one liked fair-haired men, of course, and did not have one's eyes bemused by tall, thin, black-haired ones.

'Where do you live?' he asked.

She gave him her address in Knightsbridge.

'Your father is an oil executive, I believe,' he said.

'How do you know?'

'We know all about Bank personnel.'

'I don't work for the Bank,' she pointed out.

'You do,' he corrected. 'Whenever Miss Gould supplies us with a cook she gives us a curriculum vitae. I know everything about you—almost.'

'It's the last word that counts,' she retorted.

'I'm ready to put that to rights.' He negotiated his way past a van. 'That was an invitation, Miss Jones. I would like to take you out one evening.'

Miranda hesitated, not sure if she wanted to become involved with someone who worked for the Lothian Bank. On the other hand, as she was committed to work for Blaize Jefferson in a couple of weeks' time, it was silly to draw the line now.

'I would like to go out with you,' she said gravely.

'Then let's arrange it now. What are you doing over the weekend?'

'I'm already going out.'

'I thought you might be,' he said regretfully. 'Tell me when you're free and I'll try and make myself available.'

'Tuesday night.'

'Excellent. Would you like to see a show?'

She nodded and they discussed various plays until they reached the block of flats where Barbara lived.

'Till Tuesday,' Alan Watson said. 'I'll collect you here at seven-thirty.'

'Is *he* the one?' Barbara asked when Miranda told her she was going out with one of the Lothian Bank directors.

'What's that supposed to mean?' Miranda was sitting at her dressing table brushing her hair, a bright blue silk kimono wrapped around her.

'Well, I'm prepared to bet you're keen on someone at the Bank, and if you're going out with this Alan Watson. . . .'

'It's nothing like that,' Miranda said hastily.

'You mean he isn't the one.'

'There isn't a one to be the one!'

'Then how come that every day you work at the Bank you put on a different dress and make yourself up as if you were going to a photographic session? Or is it that you fancy the butler?'

Miranda gave a forced laugh. 'You should keep your imagination for your cuisine, Barbara old girl.'

'O.K. I'll mind my own business,' Barbara said. 'I know when I'm being given the brush-off.' Grinning to show she did not mind, she went out, and Miranda stared at her reflection and tried not to see mocking hazel eyes below straight black brows.

Her evening with Alan Watson was far nicer than she had expected. He was an easy man to be with and had the assurance of someone who was used to success. The play he

53

took her to see was an absorbing political drama which gave them plenty to discuss during their dinner in an expensively fashionable Mayfair restaurant. It was midnight when they drove home and, as she knew he would, he asked to see her again.

'I'm busy for the rest of the week,' she said truthfully, 'and on Friday I'm going down to Sussex.'

'I know,' he said. 'It will give me a great opportunity to see you. I'll be there for the weekend,' he explained. 'What time are you planning to get there?'

'Friday afternoon. I won't be taking over in the kitchen until Saturday.'

'Then it doesn't matter to you what time you arrive.' At her nod he added: 'How about letting me drive you down? I'll be leaving London about five.'

She accepted the offer at once. 'How far is the house from the sea?' she asked.

'About ten minutes by car. You have to drive down the cliff road. But there's a swimming pool in the gardens. I'm sure Blaize will let you use it.'

Miranda was not quite as sure, but refrained from saying so.

'I'll wait downstairs for you in the lobby,' she said. 'Try not to be later than five. I'd like to get settled in and have a talk with the other cook.'

'Mrs. Holden is a poppet,' he said. 'She's been with Blaize for years; worked for his parents, in fact.' Alan looked down at Miranda with a tender expression. 'She'll be surprised when she gets her first glimpse of you. I doubt if you're anyone's idea of a chef—more likely a chefette!'

Miranda pulled a face at him and he caught hold of her and kissed her quickly on the lips.

'Till Friday,' he said huskily, and returned to the car.

Going up in the elevator Miranda would have given a great deal to know if Blaize Jefferson knew that Alan had taken her out tonight. The two men were friends and if she continued to see Alan he would be certain to mention it. It would be amusing if she could meet Blaize socially; it would be one way of making him look at her as something other than a kitchen utensil. She would try to arrange it as soon as she returned to London again. It would mean having to find out the places that Blaize Jefferson went to and then inveigle Alan into taking her there. But first she would see what happened during her week in Sussex. Excitement tingled through her and she tried to push it back, unwilling to anticipate something that might never arise.

Alan called for her as promised. He must have left the office early to change, for he had discarded his city clothes and looked considerably younger in tweeds. Though he was staid compared with the men she knew—they would have worn jeans or corduroy to drive into the country—there was something refreshing about his essentially public school behaviour. One could never imagine him losing his temper or doing anything underhand. His lip was made to be kept stiff, his eyes set on to the straight and narrow. Yet with the discarding of his city clothes he had discarded his city air and was unusually light-hearted. It was his boyishness that she liked best; this and the fact that he made no sexy innuendoes nor attempted to touch her beyond the normal helping her in and out of the car or on and off with her coat.

The drive to Sussex took slightly less than two hours, for they had left ahead of the traffic, ahead of Blaize Jefferson too who, Alan told her, would be arriving later that evening with a couple of guests.

'He's going to the airport to pick them up, so he should be home around eight-thirty.'

'He works extremely late hours,' she commented. 'It isn't good for him.'

'Try telling him that,' Alan grinned. 'If you'd like to walk around without a head, I mean!'

She laughed. 'I've already learned my lesson with Mr. Jefferson. I intend to be neither seen nor heard—just tasted!'

It was his turn to laugh. 'You're an amusing girl, Miranda. In fact the only one I know with a genuine sense of humour.'

'You must mix with the wrong kind,' she commented.

'I don't mix with any kind. I haven't had much time for women.'

'I'll send your name in to a computer dating service!'

'It's from choice,' he explained. 'I work hard and I can't be bothered going out with girls who always end by boring me.' His voice softened. 'I'm trying—rather clumsily—to say that you're different.'

Carefully she looked out of the window at the passing scene and Alan took the hint and turned the conversation to something else.

The nearer they got to the South Coast the greater grew Miranda's excitement, and she was breathless with it as they turned in through a pair of stone pillars and went down a winding drive bordered by fields which gave way to lawns as they came closer to the house.

'How many acres does Mr. Jefferson have?' she asked.

'A couple of hundred. Enough to ensure privacy.'

'No doubt,' she said drily, and stopped as the house came into view. It was everything a dream house should be: mellow, rustic and Elizabethan-looking, with its whitewashed walls and timbered façade. Elizabethan too with its lead windows, though, as they skirted the side of the house and she glimpsed the back of it, she saw that the windows here were modern with a wide expanse of glass.

'Part of the house was gutted by fire,' Alan explained, 'and when it was rebuilt Blaize decided not to copy the old part but to keep it modern. It means that the main living room gets a lot of light and also a superb view of the Downs.'

Stepping out of the car, Miranda drew her first breath of sea air, marvelling at how different it was here from London. A manservant hurried out to help with the cases and she followed Alan into a square-tiled hall and thence into a cheerful sitting room. The furniture and décor was English in style with most of the pieces being genuine antiques. Knowing that the exceptionally modern decor of the Bank had been Blaize Jefferson's choice she had not expected his home to be at such variance with it, and was delighted that it was, for modern furniture would have looked incongruous in these low-ceilinged rooms.

'Well?' Alan asked. 'Does it meet with your expectations?'

'It's even better. I was afraid everything would be modern.'

'Blaize used to have a modern house on the other side of the village. All glass and Swedish timber. But then he found this place and started renovating it, and when Ann married he moved in here and gave her his other home as a wedding present.'

'Ann?' Miranda questioned.

'His sister. She married Mark Kerr, Lord Aulderton's son. You'll be seeing her while you're here. They generally come over for a meal during the weekend.'

'I'm here as a cook, not a guest.' Miranda considered it was time to remind Alan of her position. 'You mustn't expect to see much of me while I'm here.'

'What on earth are you talking about?' he asked.

'You know very well what I'm talking about. I'm sure Mr. Jefferson doesn't expect me to socialise with his guests.'

'I didn't realise you were such a snob!' She couldn't help

laughing and Alan joined in. 'Anyway,' he continued, 'Blaize won't expect you to stick yourself in the kitchen once you've finished cooking.'

'He won't expect me to stick myself among his guests either,' she said with unusual asperity. 'Which reminds me, I'd better go to the kitchen and introduce myself.'

Alan led her down a short flight of stairs to the lower ground floor. Because of the lie of the land it was not subterranean, and the windows of the cheerful staff sitting room, butler's pantry and kitchen looked out on an old-fashioned herb garden. The same careful attention given to the upstairs part of the house had also been expended here, for though the kitchen was rustic in appearance with a scrubbed wooden table, tiled floor and pine cupboards, it had the latest gadgets, including a vast deep-freeze, and gas and electric ovens. The kitchen seemed full of people, but they quickly settled into two men and four women. The men and two women were Spanish, while the other two were English: local girls who came in daily to help Mrs. Holden, who was a plump and motherly sixty-year-old. She tried to hide her surprise at her first sight of Miranda, but was obviously discomfited to think her place was being taken by someone she obviously regarded as a slip of a girl. As she started to show Miranda round the kitchen, Miranda deliberately began to talk about food, and the cook's unease lessened.

'There are only four guests for dinner tonight,' Mrs. Holden explained, 'but I've already prepared the dinner, so you have nothing to worry about. Tomorrow there'll be eight for lunch and probably the same number in the evening. Sunday lunch there are bound to be several more people, but most of them go about tea-time and there's only Mr. Jefferson and one or two for dinner.'

'When does Mr. Jefferson return to London?' Miranda asked.

'Usually Monday morning unless he has a particularly early engagement: then he'll leave Sunday night.' The woman glanced at one of the maids. 'Maria, show Miss Jones to her bedroom, then you can come down and lay the table for dinner.' Mrs. Holden spoke to Miranda. 'I always give the staff supper beforehand. It doesn't do to have them hungry when they're serving upstairs, otherwise they tend to rush things.'

Musing that she had let herself in for more than she had anticipated, Miranda went to her room. It was going to be nerve-racking to cope with such a lot of staff and she wished she had found this out before she had accepted the job. Still, it would not have made any difference to her taking it. She would have been prepared to cook for a regiment in order to have the chance of seeing Blaize Jefferson outside of his office. The trouble was that in a house of this size, with so many guests surrounding him, she would be lucky if she saw him at all!

Her bedroom was in the staff wing, a small block which had obviously been added to the main building some years before. Everything was modern and compact, and there were some half dozen rooms, each with its own bathroom, and also a kitchen where one could make a snack when off duty. Blaize Jefferson certainly had his home life as well organised as his office life. No wonder he wasn't married. Yet a well-run house did not preclude having a wife and she was curious to know if he was single from choice or because he had not yet found the right girl. Somehow she was sure that when it came to choosing a partner his standards would be high and inflexible.

She was in the kitchen making careful note of everything Mrs. Holden was telling her, when the master of the house arrived. He was chauffeur-driven tonight in the silver-grey Rolls and, within moments of his entry, the rooms came alive with sound. There was laughter and voices from the drawing room and sounds of music wafted out on the still air, making her realise how quiet it was here without the drone of traffic.

'I'll be going very early in the morning,' Mrs. Holden broke into Miranda's thoughts, 'so I'm off to bed as soon as I've cleared here.'

'You can go now,' said Miranda. 'I'll see that everything is put away.'

Gratefully the older woman accepted the offer. She had explained that she was only taking a week's holiday because a friend of hers had unexpectedly had an operation and required a week's rest at home. 'But I wouldn't have left Mr. Jefferson in the lurch,' she said, 'though of course he insisted that I went, even before he knew you would stand in for me.'

Miranda thought it highly likely that one of the Spanish women could have cooked for him, but felt it was not politic to say so, and hid a smile when Mrs. Holden informed her that Maria had offered to take over the running of the kitchen but that she had not been prepared to let Mr. Jefferson's stomach suffer a mess of foreign food.

'Sometimes Maria goes to Soho and comes back with all sorts of weird things. Octopus and suchlike, and peppers hot enough to burn off your tongue. Good English cooking is what I do, with a bit of French from time to time, though I suppose *you*'d consider me an old-fashioned cook.'

'Most of the best cooks are,' Miranda said diplomatically, and was rewarded by a gratified sniff before Mrs. Holden wished her goodnight, left her a card with her address and phone number should an emergency arise and departed to her room.

Miranda remained in the kitchen till the dinner things had been put away and the breakfast crockery set out for the next morning. No one had breakfast in their rooms unless they were ill, José the butler informed her, and breakfast itself was set out on a hot-tray in the dining room at nine and was cleared away again at ten, though coffee was always left percolating until eleven for any exceptionally late riser. Cooking for a household was certainly more exacting than preparing luncheon in the City, Miranda thought, as she extracted frozen kidneys from the deep freeze and took the eggs out of the refrigerator to come to room temperature overnight in the kitchen. Catering for a house party like this would leave her with no free time, for as soon as one meal was over another one had to be prepared. But no doubt one got into the routine, and Mrs. Holden certainly did not look the worse for wear.

'The weekends are always busy,' José said, as if sensing what she was thinking, 'but there is nothing for us to do during the week. If Mr. Jefferson does come back he is generally alone, or maybe has one other guest. But if you need any extra help, just ask me or Miguel.'

Miranda smiled her thanks at his offer, though from the way Maria was watching him she thought it would be safer if she did not ask him for help. Spanish women were very jealous and were also very handy with a knife!

She was walking down the corridor to the servants' wing when Alan was suddenly in front of her, almost like a genie appearing from a wall.

'Hidden doors!' he exclaimed before she could ask him where he had come from. 'The house has several of them. If you're a good girl I'll take you exploring.' He caught hold of her hand. 'Come and have a stroll.'

'I'm going to bed.'

'Is that an invitation?'

'Don't be silly!' smiled Miranda.

He sighed. 'I knew you'd turn me down.' Still holding her hand, he pulled her towards a door and from there led her across the herb garden to the south side of the house. She could hear the music more clearly from here and glimpsed several figures through the windows of the drawing room.

'Blaize asked me to make sure you had everything you wanted,' he said.

'That was very kind of him,' Miranda replied formally. 'Please thank him for me.'

'Come in and thank him yourself.'

'No.' Miranda pulled back as Alan went to draw her towards the French windows.

'Why not?' Ignoring her protest, he pulled her into the drawing room, which seemed to be full of towering men.

'Good evening, Miss Jones.' It was the one man she had wanted to see and, like a schoolgirl, she stood and gawped at him, tilting her head a long way back before she was able to do so, and wishing she had remembered to wear high heels.

'I didn't know we had a female guest,' a deep American voice said. 'You told me it was strictly stag.'

'Miss Jones is our cook,' his host drawled.

'You mean she did the dinner tonight?'

'No, that was done by my permanent cook. But Miss Jones is kindly standing in for her for a week. You'll be able to sample her cuisine tomorrow.'

'If she cooks as good as she looks,' said another American, big and rangy as the first, 'then I can't wait to tuck in.'

Blaize smiled. 'It would sound uncomplimentary if I said she cooks even better than she looks, but——'

'That would be impossible,' said the first American, smiling into Miranda's eyes.

Miranda felt she was being spoken about as if she were not here, and she drew up all of her five foot two as she spoke to the man she had come to work for. 'I hope you'll tell me if any of your guests have food allergies or religious taboos?'

'None that I know of,' he replied solemnly, 'so stop looking so worried and tell me what you would like to drink.'

She considered for a moment. 'Just a coffee, I think.'

'Can't I tempt you to a liqueur? I have an excellent brandy.'

'The best, I'm sure.' She coloured. 'Sorry, that popped out.'

'Your remarks generally do,' he said dryly.

'Only with you. There's something about the way you make your statements that provokes me.'

'I'm a very provoking man,' he said so gravely that she knew he was teasing her. It gave her a heady feeling, and as she accepted the cup of coffee she gave him a more natural smile.

'I hear that Alan drove you down,' he said.

'Yes, I hope you didn't mind.'

'Why should I?'

'Well, he's a friend of yours and I'm working for you, so——'

'Alan works for me, too.'

'I didn't mean that.'

'I know what you meant, Miss Jones, and I'm trying to tell you that you're foolish.'

'Alan said the same,' she confessed.

'Then at least listen to him if you won't listen to me.'

'Well, Miranda,' said Alan, coming to stand beside her. 'It isn't such an ordeal, is it?' Before she could answer he looked at Blaize. 'The silly girl didn't want to come in here in case you objected.'

Hazel eyes, more grey than green tonight, moved over Miranda's face. 'I asked Alan down for the weekend in order to see something of him, but if you object to mixing with us, he'll be spending his time in the kitchen!'

'When you put it like that, Mr. Jefferson, I can't refuse to come in,' said Miranda.

'Good.' He glanced from her to Alan and then moved over to the two Americans. Miranda hid her disappointment that he had gone away so quickly, and then cheered herself up with the knowledge that he probably thought he was doing her a favour by leaving her alone with Alan. But he mustn't be allowed to think she was interested in his friend; that would spoil everything.

'I suppose you're going to be busy for the whole of tomorrow morning,' Alan said quietly.

'I'll be busy all day,' she replied. 'Despite what Mr. Jefferson says, I can't come in here and socialise. I've been brought here to do a job and I'm going to be tied up the whole weekend.'

'Then I'll drive down and see you during the week.'

'I'll be in town the week after. You talk as if I'll be away for years.'

'It will be years to me.'

'Do stop flirting, Alan!' she begged.

'Why?'

'Because I don't want you to.' She hesitated and then said more bluntly: 'I just want us to be friends.'

'You aren't embarrassed because Blaize is here, are you?' His eyes narrowed. 'He already knows I've taken you out.'

Before she could reply Blaize Jefferson strolled back to them carrying his empty coffee cup and, seeing Miranda had drunk hers, he held out his hand for it. She gave it to him and, nervous of touching his fingers, withdrew her hand from the saucer before he had firmly grasped it. Cup and saucer seemed momentarily suspended in the air and then dropped to the floor with a crash.

'Damn!' he said, and bent to pick it up.

Miranda bent too and the contact she had been trying to avoid occurred now as, reaching for the broken cup, she grasped his finger with it.

Smiling slightly, he extricated his hand. 'I'm sorry, Miss

Jones, I don't normally drop things.'

'It was my fault,' she mumbled and, straightening with the broken china, thought this as good a time as any to make her departure. She said goodnight and gave Alan such a determined look that he took the hint and did not offer to come with her to the kitchen.

A little later, lying in bed in her room, she heard voices softly speaking in the garden and knew that Blaize Jefferson was strolling there with his guests. It was an effort to stop herself from going to the window and peering out at him, but she refused to give in to the longing and pulled the bedclothes firmly around her head. She was acting like a teenager with a crush, instead of a mature young lady with a mind of her own.

CHAPTER FIVE

MIRANDA was correct in her assertion that she would be busy the entire weekend. Beginning with a cooked breakfast of kidneys, bacon and coddled eggs, she went on to prepare a three-course lunch and a four-course dinner. During the interim she whipped up a batch of cakes and some ice cream and by nine o'clock that evening was exhausted and ready for bed. She retired there immediately coffee had been served, determined to do so before Alan could seek her out, and missing him, so José told her on Sunday morning, by the skin of her teeth. This was echoed by Alan who came into the kitchen at nine-thirty to say good morning.

'If Mohammed won't come to the mountain. . . .' he said, and finished the sentence by giving her a hug.

'I wasn't avoiding you,' she lied, 'but I really have been busy.'

'Then I'll stay here and keep you company. I'm a dab

hand with a potato.'

'Susan does the vegetables.' She pointed to one of the local girls. 'And today isn't going to be as bad. I'm serving a roast for lunch and left-overs for supper.'

'Even your left-overs are better than anyone else's beginnings!' He licked his lips. 'What is it?'

'Fillet of beef and apple pie. Now be a dear and leave me alone.'

'Blaize wondered if you would like to join us for morning coffee and a swim.'

'Doesn't Blaize have a tongue of his own?' she queried.

'Yes,' said an amused voice, 'when Alan gives me a chance to use it!'

Alan went scarlet and so did Miranda, as Blaize Jefferson strolled into the kitchen.

'Do you always sneak up on people?' she demanded.

'I can hardly be described as sneaking up in my own house,' he said mildly, and gave his friend a grin. 'Thanks for inviting Miss Jones for a swim. As a matter of fact I had come in to do it myself.'

'Sorry, old chap.' Alan mumbled something inaudible and disappeared.

'Now you've embarrassed him,' Miranda said crossly.

'He deserves to be embarrassed for making me sound like a halfwit.'

'He was just trying to make me feel welcome.'

'And not succeeding, from the sound of what you said. Though I don't blame you for being a bit sharp about it, Miss Jones. After all, an invitation from one's host should come from the host himself.'

'I don't regard you as my host,' Miranda said, embarrassed. 'I'm here as a cook and you're my employer.'

'That's still no reason why you can't come and have a swim. I take it you do swim?'

'I jump off at the deep end too.'

He chuckled. 'With both feet, I should imagine!'

She laughed. 'My friends call me impulsive and my enemies headstrong.'

'I should imagine you're both.'

She nodded, and seeing Susan looking at her, signalled the girl to start chopping the carrots that glistened golden on one of the draining boards.

'We'll expect you about eleven, then, Miss Jones,' Blaize Jefferson said, and walked out before she could answer him.

The next hour flew by with wings and Miranda worked with the speed of two. It was amazing how lighthearted happiness could make one feel and she was bubbling with it as she went to her room to slip on a swimsuit. She had brought her three prettiest ones with her, but because of the two Americans, one of whom had a distinctly roving eye, she chose her least scanty bikini, and wore a matching shirt with it. It was in aquamarine silk, a colour almost identical with her eyes which were sparkling with pleasure, tilted and provocative. She eyed herself in the mirror, uncertain at showing so much of herself. There certainly seemed to be a large expanse of silky skin between the top of her bikini and the beginning of the brief pants, but her curves were delightful and there was not an ounce of superfluous fat to be seen. Coming to the conclusion that if it were not for Blaize Jefferson she would not be embarrassed at all, she slipped on espadrilles and flapped her way across the lawn to the pool.

Four pairs of male eyes watched her approach and the embarrassment she had denied in her bedroom washed over her in full flood. As always it made her talk too much. 'I feel like Daniel entering the lions' den.' She sat down quickly on a mattress, wishing she could lie under it instead of on it. One of the Americans obligingly gave a roar while the other growled.

'If you eat me,' she said brightly, 'you won't get any lunch.'

'If I eat you,' said Hank, the youngest of the Americans, 'I won't want any lunch!' His friend and Alan both laughed; only Blaize Jefferson looked unamused and Miranda wondered if he was annoyed at her attire. He was in white shorts which made his skin look more bronzed. He had certainly not acquired that colour in English sunshine.

'Have you been on holiday recently?' she asked him.

'Blaize's life is one long holiday,' said Hank. 'He just combines it with business from time to time!'

'The other way round,' Blaize retorted, and answered Miranda's question by a nod. 'I was in St. Tropez last weekend.' He eyed her. 'You obviously haven't been away.'

She stared with disfavour at her creamy skin. 'I do look a bit ghostly, don't I?'

'You look fabulous.' Alan came into the conversation, rolling over on his stomach to do so. He was in shorts too, his fair hair ruffled and already wet from a swim. 'Most girls with such black hair have an olive skin. Yours is like a camellia.' He touched one curving thigh and she jumped up quickly.

'Anyone for a swim?' The moment she spoke she regretted her words, for it drew all eyes towards her again, and they remained glued on her as she took off her shirt and stood revealed.

'Wow!' said Hank. 'How many beauty competitions have you won?'

'Hundreds. I was Miss Pork Chop last year!' she said flippantly and, running to the edge of the water, dived cleanly into it.

The one thing Miranda did well was swim. She had learned in the warm waters of the Persian Gulf and had never lost her sensuous pleasure in feeling water lap against her skin. The pool was heated, but it still had a tingling freshness and she swam for several yards underwater and then did a leisurely crawl to the far end of the pool and a slow breast-stroke back. By this time the two Americans had joined her and Alan sat up to watch them. Only Blaize Jefferson still remained aloof, standing near the edge of the pool, a copy of the *Sunday Times* in his hand as if he had not made up his mind whether to read the paper or not.

Holding on to the tiled edge, Miranda let her feet float upwards to the surface and her hair splayed out around her like strands of black satin. Her eyes were on a level with his feet and she was intensely aware of the firm muscles of his legs and the way they tensed along the back of his calves. He was not looking in her direction but was speaking to Alan and moving slightly on his heels as he did so. A couple of ants scurried along the tiled surround of the pool and then a darker striped yellow body followed: a huge hornet, furry and ferocious. Alan murmured something and Blaize Jefferson moved again. His feet lifted, the hornet moved beneath them and as his feet went to come down again, Miranda screamed. The man jerked back sharply, one foot slipped on the edge of the pool and the other rose in the air. For a split second he seemed poised as though held motionless by invisible strings, then he flopped down into the water, sending up a cascade of spray. Wet sheets of newspaper spread out on the surface of the pool and then slowly sank to the bottom while Blaize recovered his equilibrium, lunged for the side of the pool and then glared at her.

'If that's your idea of a joke, Miss Jones——'

'Treading on a hornet is no joke!'

'What hornet?'

'The one you nearly trod on.' She looked for it, but the tiled surround was bare, save for footmarks. 'There was a huge hornet there,' she assured him, 'and you were just about to put your foot on it when I screamed. I thought you would prefer to get wet than stung.' She remembered the

69

ignominious way he had fallen into the water, arms thrashing round his head, expression indignant, and could not stop a giggle escaping her.

At the sound, his look of irritation returned and she knew that he thought she was lying.

'I am not,' she said crossly.

'Not what?'

'Lying.'

'Oh?' One dark eyebrow rose higher than the other. 'You have the most weird habit of talking at random.'

'It isn't at random,' she explained. 'I just think of half of something and say the rest out loud.'

'I'm beginning to realise that. At times it makes your conversation a little difficult to follow.'

'My father says I might madden a man to death, but I'll never bore him to it.'

There was a moment of silence. 'Your father is a man of perspicacity, Miss Jones.' With a lithe movement he heaved himself from the water and stood on the edge, skin glistening brown, hair even blacker now that it was wet. He looked such a magnificent specimen of manhood that she was overwhelmed by it and she sank to the bottom of the pool and busied herself gathering the sheets of sodden newspaper. She surfaced with them in her hand and placed a squelchy mess on the side.

'The political news is always wet anyway,' she said, and burst out laughing. Alan and the two Americans joined in, though Blaize Jefferson did not do so. Silently he picked up the paper and took it over to lay it on the lawn.

'I think I've outstayed my welcome,' Miranda whispered to Alan as she joined him on the mattress and reached out for a towel.

'You saved him from a very nasty sting.'

'You saw the hornet too?'

'Only as it flew away.'

'I wish you'd told him. He thinks I did it on purpose to make him fall in the pool.'

Alan looked astonished and before Miranda could stop him, shouted out: 'Miranda wasn't lying, Blaize, you nearly *did* tread on a hornet. I saw it as it flew off.'

Quickly Miranda slipped on her shirt and sped across the grass, but she had only gone a few yards when a hand came out and gripped her shoulder.

'This is the second apology I have to make to you.'

Miranda did not need to look round to know who was speaking. 'That's quite all right. In your place I would probably have thought the same.'

'No, you wouldn't.' His voice was unexpectedly humorous. 'You're such an honest little thing you would believe the best of everybody.'

At this she turned. 'You talk as if I'm a fool!'

'Only in the nicest possible way.' His hand dropped from her shoulder. 'Don't get too wise, Miss Jones, you're very nice as you are.'

Miranda hugged the words to her as though each one was a pearl. She kept reading different meanings into the remark: one moment seeing it as a compliment, the next as a brilliant assessment of her character and then as a light-hearted attempt at flirtation. But when she saw him again later that afternoon he was as coolly aloof towards her as always, though he unbent sufficiently to introduce her to his sister and brother-in-law who had arrived for tea.

'So you're the sensational cook Blaize has been talking about?' Ann Kerr was the exact physical opposite of her brother, being small, plump and fair, though her plumpness, she confided as her brother and husband moved away, was due to three-month-old Mark junior, sleeping contentedly in his nursery a mile away. 'It's because of him that I'm supposed to be on a diet,' she said, munching on a cake.

'But I'm afraid I succumbed. How long have you been cooking?'

'Professionally for a year. Before that I trained with Madam Elise.'

'What a wonderful idea!'

'I wasn't brainy,' Miranda admitted, 'and I would never have got into university—whereas I love cooking.'

'Which is much more useful than a dull old degree. I lunched at the Bank a few weeks ago when your predecessor was there, but Blaize says you're heaps better.'

Miranda was surprised that cookery should be a subject discussed between brother and sister, and as if knowing what she was thinking, Ann said: 'Blaize adores his food. I always say he's a sucker for anything that appeals to his eye or his stomach—but then, most sensual men like food and wine.'

'I don't see Mr. Jefferson in quite that light.'

'Don't be fooled by his austere manner. It hides a quick temper and a passionate nature.'

'I know about the temper,' Miranda said so promptly that the other girl laughed.

'What's the joke?' her brother asked, coming over to join them again.

'I've been hearing about your temper,' said Ann.

'From Tactless Tilly?' Blaize Jefferson said.

For an instant his sister was startled, then she laughed again, but at Miranda this time, who felt her cheeks go pink. 'What your brother is trying to say, Mrs. Kerr, is that whenever I open my mouth, he puts his foot in it!'

'Which, when translated,' Blaize Jefferson continued, 'means I have an unhappy tendency to arrive unheralded just when Miss Jones is saying something charming about me!'

'You two should work out a better communication system,' Ann giggled, and her grey-green eyes, the only similarity between brother and sister, swivelled round to Miranda. 'I'm sure Blaize is exaggerating. I bet you're just being truthful with him, but because all the women he knows always flatter him, he considers *you* tactless!'

'I would like to agree with you,' Miranda smiled, 'but unfortunately your brother is right.' From the corner of her eye she saw he had moved away again and was disappointed until she realised that the two Americans were preparing to leave. She wondered with dismay whether he was going to drive them to London, and it was only when Hank was saying goodbye to her that she learned Alan was taking them.

'I hope we meet again soon,' he said, pumping her hand as if it were one of the oil wells she knew he owned. 'If you give me your number I'll call you and fix a date.'

'I'm living here for the moment,' she replied.

'Next time I'm in town, then,' said Hank, and she watched him go, grateful that her excuse for not seeing him was a good one. Then Alan came over to say goodbye and though she knew he wanted to draw her away from Ann Kerr, she resolutely remained where she was, a fact which he interpreted by bestowing a wry look on her.

'You won't always escape me,' he murmured as he kissed her cheek. 'I'll be seeing you, Miranda,' he said out loud. 'Next weekend, probably.'

'What a lovely name you have,' Ann commented when the two of them were alone again. 'It's so unusual. But then you are unusual. Capable and beautiful. It's a rare combination.'

'You're too complimentary. Anyway, you've only tasted my cakes.'

'I'll come over for lunch one day this week. Blaize says you'll be here until Mrs. Holden returns.'

Miranda was pleased that she would not be left entirely to her own devices during the coming week.

'Blaize was lucky that you agreed to help him out,' Ann went on. 'If I were single I wouldn't want to stick myself in the country.'

'It's only for ten days,' Miranda said, and stopped speaking as Mark Kerr joined them. Like his wife he was fair and plump and seemed equally good-natured. They chatted for a few moments and then left, with Ann reiterating her promise to join her for lunch during the week.

Aware that when Blaize Jefferson came back from bidding goodbye to his guests, she would be alone with him, Miranda went hastily to the kitchen. If he wanted to be with her, he could come in search of her.

One of the Spanish couples had gone off for the evening, leaving José and his wife, who told her that when Mr. Jefferson was alone he had supper on a tray in the library. 'I have already set the tray for him,' José said, 'and if you wish I can prepare the salad.'

Thanking him but shaking her head, Miranda set about doing so herself. She had made some chicken liver paté and she piled it up in a golden brown mound ready to be served with hot buttered toast. This was to be followed by a creamy mushroom soup.

'But the master always has a cold supper,' José said.

'It's become a bit chilly,' Miranda explained, 'and a cold meal can be depressing to eat on your own.' She poured the soup into a pan and set it on the electric hob. The salad lay green and inviting in a beautiful teak bowl, something which its owner had brought back from one of his jaunts abroad, as he had no doubt brought many of the things she had seen around the house. She glanced at her watch, then asked José what time Sunday supper was served.

'I don't know,' he said. 'Because it is always a cold meal on Sunday, I put it in the library and the master serves himself.'

Miranda frowned. 'You'd better ask him what time he

74

would like it.'

José hurried away, returning after a moment to give her a strange look. 'Mr. Jefferson says would you please go to the drawing room.'

Avoiding the butler's curious eyes, she obeyed the summons, pausing outside the drawing room door to smooth her hair and tighten the belt of her dress, a simple one in creamy silk with a fitted bodice and pleated skirt.

Blaize was pouring himself a drink as she came in and he poured a second drink and brought it over to her. It was a Martini, ice cold and very dry, and she sipped it and shuddered.

'Too much gin?'

'Any gin is too much. I loathe it.'

'Sorry.' He took the glass from her. 'Sweet sherry, perhaps?'

'Bitter lemon.'

He smiled. 'You know you don't mean that.'

'Vodka, actually.'

'That tastes of nothing,' he pointed out.

'That's how I like my alcohol. I don't drink for the taste, only for the effect!'

His eyebrows rose. 'And what effect does alcohol have on you, Miss Jones?'

'You'll have to wait and find out, Mr. Jefferson.'

For the first time the twitch of his lips curved into a proper grin. 'I think we can dispense with formalities now, don't you, Miranda?'

She nodded, knowing she would find it difficult to say his name. He poured her the drink she had requested and brought it back, together with some tonic which he added until she signalled him to stop. He had given her a large vodka, but she did not comment on it and hoped her head would stand her in good stead.

'I expect you to have supper with me tonight,' he said,

sitting down and stretching his legs out in front of him. 'It's pointless for us to eat alone.'

'I'll be eating with José and Maria,' she told him.

'Thanks,' he said drily. 'Do I take it you would prefer that?'

'Of course not,' she said instantly. 'I would love to have supper with you. But I don't want you to ask me because you thought I might be lonely.'

His eyebrows rose again. 'It never entered my mind that you would be lonely. You strike me as being far too self-sufficient for that.'

'I seem to strike you in a lot of different ways.'

'You do,' he agreed, 'but so far, not with your hands! I must confess I've never met anyone as mercurial and changeable. I was thinking over what your father said about you. He's completely right. You might exasperate a man to death, but you'd never bore him to it!'

'If I need a testimonial I'll know where to come,' she smiled.

He laughed and cupped his glass in his hands. 'How is it you aren't already married? I'd have thought a girl like you would be snapped up. I mean, they do say that the way to a man's heart is through his stomach.'

'These days it's much more likely to be through his bedroom!'

He gave her a searching look. 'Isn't that something one takes for granted these days?'

'Some people do. I'm one of the few who don't.'

'Thank heavens you aren't one of the don't knows,' he said drily.

'Never a don't know,' she replied. 'If anything I'm always too positive in my reactions.'

'So am I, and it isn't a good thing. It's better if one is malleable, then one can adjust with the times and the situation.'

'I'm sure you *do* adjust,' she said. 'I think that's the reason for your success.'

He looked down into his drink. 'I can make adjustments in my business life,' he said slowly, 'but I find it more difficult to do so in my personal life.' Abruptly he drained his glass and stood up. 'A refill?' he asked and, as she shook her head, filled his own glass, but he did not sit down again. Miranda had the feeling that their conversation had brought back memories he wished to forget and again she wondered why he was not married.

'What time would you like supper?' she asked. His soft laugh made her look at him. 'What have I said that's funny?'

'Nothing. But you were sitting there looking incredibly beautiful—you really do have the most astonishing colouring—and I imagined you were thinking ethereal thoughts when all the time you were concerned about meat and spuds.'

'Liver paté and mushroom soup, actually.'

'How literal you are!'

'Only in self-defence.'

'Self-defence?' He swooped on the words as he swooped on her, taking the glass in one hand and pulling her up with the other. 'You don't need to put up any barriers with me, Miranda Jones. I'm harmless.'

'Like a barracuda.'

'Not a fish,' he said plaintively. 'You know I'm allergic to them!'

She giggled. 'I'm sorry, I forgot.'

'Don't,' he said seriously, 'it could kill me.'

Discomfited, she put a hand up towards him, as though to touch his cheek. 'I wouldn't like to do that,' she said huskily.

'I'm sure you wouldn't.' His eyes looked into hers. 'I think we'll have supper now, don't you?'

Not trusting herself to speak, she pulled her hand away from his and left the room. She would have liked to change into something more exotic, but knew that if she did he would assume she was trying to make herself look attractive to him. More attractive, she amended, for she was sure he was well aware of her as a woman. No one could have been with the two Americans today and not been aware of it, for their admiration had been open and verbal. She was glad Alan had driven them back to London, otherwise she would never have had the chance of being alone with Blaize. Elated at the prospect, she made the toast, wrapped it in a napkin to keep it hot, then poured the bubbling mushroom soup into a tureen and set it on the tray. José carried it into the library for her and placed it on a small table set up by the window.

Sitting opposite Blaize and staring through the wide expanse of glass at the beautifully lit swimming pool twenty yards away, Miranda appreciated the merits of a picture window compared with the small, leaded panes in the rest of the house.

'Excellent paté, this,' the man opposite her said.

'Wait till you try the soup,' she smiled. 'It's my speciality.'

'I'm sure you say that about all the dishes you make!'

She laughed and bit into a creamy mound of chicken liver. Expecting to feel ill at ease, she was surprised at how relaxed she was in this lovely book-lined room with its tall, black-haired owner only a couple of feet away. Blaize looked more relaxed too, and when she shyly commented on it, he agreed.

'I had some pretty tough bargaining to do with Hank and to begin with he wasn't prepared to give a thing away.'

'Was the weekend here a softening-up process?' she asked.

'You can't soften up a man like Hank. I was trying to

78

show him I was a relaxed country gentleman who didn't care whether I got his business or not.'

'Did you succeed?'

'Of course.'

'How silly of me to ask!' She cleared the first set of dishes and poured the soup into bowls. 'Does he have any other business apart from his oil wells?'

'A newspaper chain and television station; supermarkets —about a hundred or so—and a huge machine tool company.' One eyebrow quirked. 'Don't tell me you're interested in business as well as cooking?'

'I'm interested in everything.'

'Isn't that what mothers teach their daughters? To provide a good table and a sympathetic ear until the ring is on the third finger?'

She was so angry that it was an effort to speak calmly. 'As you're extremely unlikely to put a ring on *my* finger, don't you think you're being rather cynical?'

'I guess old fears die hard.'

'Fears?'

'Matchmaking mamas consider me a good catch,' he said abruptly. 'I'm used to having bait dangled in front of me.'

'What stopped you from biting it—or were you always a wary fish?'

His lids lowered and it was as if shutters had come down over his face. 'Some more wine?' he asked, and she accepted this as his way of ending the discussion.

'If you won't be coming down until the weekend, Blaize, it seems silly for me to stay here by myself,' she said.

'Do you have any special reason for wanting to be in London?'

'No.'

'Then why not stay here and take advantage of the good weather? Look on it as a holiday.'

'But you're paying me,' she pointed out.

'My dear girl,' he seemed faintly exasperated and she had the uncomfortable sensation that in referring to money she had mentioned the unmentionable. 'I may come down one evening during the week,' he continued. 'It depends if I can get away early.'

'You work too hard,' she said.

'I like it.' He sampled her soup. 'Delicious! You must give this recipe to Mrs. Holden—unless you keep it secret.'

'The way most women won't tell you the name of their dressmaker?' she smiled. 'I'm not like that. I'll give Mrs. Holden any of the recipes you like.'

'You're a creature of all virtues, Miranda. Don't you have any vices?'

'None I'm prepared to speak of.'

He chuckled and at the same time reached for his wine glass. It tipped and amber green hock stained the white cloth. Swiftly he dabbed it with his napkin. 'I know one thing that you are,' he said, half amused, half irritated. 'A jinx. Whenever you're around I always do something ridiculous.'

'You can't blame me because you're clumsy,' Miranda protested.

'The one thing I am *not* is clumsy,' he said emphatically. 'But there is something about you.... First I dropped that coffee cup on Friday; next you made me fall into the pool, and now this. Do you always have such an effect on the men in your life?'

'Never.'

He poured himself some more wine and sipped it as if to restore his humour. 'Are there many men?'

'Lots,' she said, 'but only friends.'

'Is Alan one of them?'

'I like to think so.' She kept her voice light and wondered if his question stemmed from interest or curiosity.

'Alan is a good chap,' he said, 'you could do worse.'

'Worse than what?' she said so sharply that he gave her a swift look and did not pursue his thoughts.

'Would you like coffee now or later?' she asked.

'Now. Then you can sit and relax.'

Not bothering to ring for José, Miranda wheeled the trolley into the kitchen and found that the butler had already prepared the coffee. Taking the tray to the library, she served it and curled up in a corner of the settee.

'You look like a little girl when you sit that way,' Blaize commented. 'I'm surprised your parents were happy to go abroad and leave you alone.'

'You keep talking as if I'm a child!'

'It's because you're so petite.'

'You keep saying that, too.'

He frowned. 'You make me sound very repetitive.' She opened her mouth and then closed it again. He saw the movement and laughed. 'I see you're learning to control your tactless comments.' He set down his cup and strolled over to the hi-fi equipment that stood along part of one wall. He pressed a button and the soft strains of violins filled the air. 'Wallpaper music,' he murmured. 'I don't feel in the mood for anything more.'

She saw this as indication of his fatigue and was uncertain whether to go or stay. She went to rise, but he had already returned to the settee and he pushed her gently back on to it and then sat beside her.

'Relax,' he murmured. 'You've been working hard this weekend too.' He lifted one of her hands. It was small in his long-fingered one, and his thumb and forefinger moved to span her wrist, doing it so easily that they overlapped.

Awareness of his touch set her heart pounding in her ears. How unconcerned he looked, sitting beside her; tall and dark and quiet; his hair ruffled at the back, the ends stopping just short of his collar. He was wearing an open-necked silk shirt, cream like the colour of her dress, and through its fine fabric she noticed the dark hair that splayed across his chest. She wished she could run her hands through it or rest her cheek against it. She wished he would pull her into his arms and hold her. She wished he would kiss her. Oh, lord, she wondered, what's happening to me?

'Relax,' Blaize repeated, and reaching out, pulled her into the crook of his arm.

With a sigh she did as he said, resting her head against his shoulder and allowing the warmth of his body to seep into hers. There was no awareness in his touch, his arm remaining across her shoulder as if she were no more than a cushion, and in an odd way she felt that she was: it was as if he needed the comfort of someone to hold, and though she would have liked him to have been aware of her, she was content just to be close to him. The music changed and the violins were replaced by harps. Suddenly she was afraid that if she remained here, she would give herself away. She pulled out of his hold and he turned his head towards her. It brought his face closer and his eyes stared into hers. His hand became heavier on her shoulder and his fingers were warm on the side of her neck.

'Don't go,' he said, and bent forward until his lips were on hers.

Their touch was soft and she trembled violently with nerves. His response to this was to hold her more firmly and turn her body fully round until she was close against him.

'I won't hurt you, Miranda. Don't be afraid of me.'

She wondered what he would say if she told him she was afraid of herself. One of her arms lifted tentatively to touch the side of his face. His cheek was firm under her fingertips, the hair at his temples thicker than she had imagined and far softer. It was almost as if she were touching satin. He moved slightly and kissed the tip of her nose, then lightly ran his lips down the side of her cheek, pausing as they reached the corner of her mouth, before coming to rest there. She felt the warmth of his breath and the slow rise and fall of his chest. How confident he was, showing none of the nervousness she was feeling. She was annoyed with herself for not being sophisticated enough to appear unconcerned. After all, there was nothing so momentous in being kissed. These days it was an all too frequent end to an evening.

His hands moved down her back, bringing her body close to his. Through his shirt there exuded the warmth of his body. It made her conscious of his closeness and the fact that he was half lying on top of her, the weight of his thigh heavy upon hers. The buckle of his trouser belt was hard against her hip bone and she trembled again, a convulsive movement that made him tighten his hold, as though by so doing he could reassure her.

'It's like holding a bird.' The thickness of his voice indicated the passion he was feeling and he half raised himself and cupped either side of her face with his hands. His eyes looked deep into hers. The pupils were enlarged, and the hazel was only a rim. Then his lids lowered and his head came down until his lips were once again on hers. This time their pressure was firmer, the kiss deeper and longer, as if he had finally given way to his emotion.

Miranda had no chance to resist him and would not have done so even if she could. Her trembling ceased and she pressed herself closer to him, enthralled by the weight of his body and the increasing pressure of his mouth. He had no need to force her lips apart, for they opened willingly beneath his, and with slow deliberation he accepted the surrender, as if he were afraid she would suddenly draw back again. But as she moved closer still his grip tightened and his kiss became deeper. Heat radiated from him and his shirt was damp. He was no longer the sardonically intense man who both attracted and frightened her. Instead he was a trembling boy, young despite his years, defenceless despite his muscular strength. She pressed her hands on the back of his head and then ran her fingers through the thick hair. Her heart was pounding in her ears and her breasts ached as the weight of his body flattened them. But she was reluctant to push him away in case he saw it as a gesture of repudiation. Instead she wriggled slightly beneath him and the soft cushions on the settee stirred against her back. The movement disturbed him and he held himself away from her, propping his weight on his arm. His lids lifted and Miranda saw that the pupils were still wide and enlarged. It made his eyes look blank and though they were staring at her, she had the impression that they were sightless, as if they were gazing inward at a picture in his mind. If they were, then the picture displeased him, for his lips were now clenched, the full lower one tightening and thinning, the softness of his jawline hardening. It was as if a metamorphosis had come over him and she knew that the immediate past had been forgotten, buried beneath the anguish of a deeper more bitter past.

Blaize straightened completely and stood up. It was not his usual lithe movement but a jerky one, and showed her that he was not as physically unmoved by what had happened as he was striving to appear. "If he tells me he's sorry," she thought dejectedly, "I'll walk out here and now."

But he did no such thing. Instead he leaned one elbow on the mantelshelf and half-turned to look at her as she lay on the settee. 'You're very desirable, Miranda. I hadn't realised I was still so susceptible.'

''Still?' she echoed. 'Why shouldn't you be? You aren't an octogenarian!'

'I wish to heaven I were. It would solve a lot of my problems.'

'So would a woman!' she said tartly, frayed nerves getting the better of her.

His mouth lifted cynically. 'Women bring complications that I can do without.'

She stood up, smoothing her dress. 'You'd better take a glass of hot milk last thing at night!'

'What about the day?' His constraint was going and humour was replacing it. 'I wanted to put my arms around you quite a few times this weekend. I can't go around all day sipping hot milk!'

Although she was pleased that humour was dissolving their embarrassment, she wished he would show a sense of regret. To be able to make a joke of their embrace implied a shallowness that made it nothing more than a purely physical need without any of the deeper implications it had held for herself.

'Well?' he questioned. 'Any other bright suggestion?'

'Try dolls,' she snapped. 'You've made it all too clear you don't want a real woman!'

She spun round to go out and her silk skirt swirled around her. He caught hold of the material to prevent her moving away.

'Please let me go,' she said in a tight voice.

'You don't need to run off,' he said softly. 'I won't do it again.'

'I won't give you the opportunity.' She pulled free of him and her heels clicked across the parquet floor.

She did not look round to say goodnight but went out, closing the door carefully behind her. She wanted to cry, yet tears would not come. In fact she was astonished that she felt no emotion. It was as if her mind had put itself into limbo and suspended time. But the clock would start again and feeling would return, and when it did she would remember tonight with bitterness and salt tears.

CHAPTER SIX

BLAIZE left early the next morning without Miranda having an opportunity to see him. He did not leave word to say if he would be coming down during the week and she wondered how she was going to keep herself occupied. The staff were friendly, but she had little in common with them, and after preparing the lunch she was left with the rest of the day free.

It was sunny, but a breeze was whipping in from the sea, making it uncomfortable to sit by the pool for long, and though she swam several lengths in order to give herself some physical exercise, once she clambered out she had to go to her room to change into warm slacks and sweater. It became colder still in the evening, and she watched television in the staff sitting room and went to bed early.

Tuesday followed a similar pattern, but after taking a swim in the early afternoon she went for an exploratory walk over the land Blaize owned. It took in a large stretch of grassland and she saw a few sheep grazing and wondered if they belonged to the estate. She glimpsed men working in the grounds near to the house, but did not know if there were any more. The further she walked the stronger became the smell of the sea and she could see it on the horizon, a shimmering sparkle too far away to have any colour. She wondered if Blaize had a boat and could imagine him at the helm, fighting the elements and winning, the way he appeared to do in his business life. Had he always been so ambitious? Certainly he could not have reached his position so young unless he were; and what had he forgone in the process? There was so much about his background that she longed to know that it made her restless, and this restlessness drove her back to the house where Maria and Iñez were cleaning the downstairs rooms.

The library was already finished and Miranda decided to sit there. She found it the most pleasant room in the house, though this was probably because it held the strongest impression of its owner. The smell of the leather-bound books was reminiscent of his after-shave lotion, an elusive yet crisp fragrance, and she glanced along the shelves to see what he read. There were the expected sets of Dickens, Scott and Thackeray, as well as many of the better known Russian classics, and a complete shelf of economic and political books, many of them American. On the wall nearest to the hi-fi were books much more to her liking: the works of Shakespeare and a selection of French classics. She leafed through a Balzac, then reaching out for another one, saw that a slim grey volume had slipped to the back. She fished it out. It was the poems of Rupert Brooke, and from the look of the cover had been well read. Opening it, she saw the initials B.H.J. on the fly leaf. The ink was faded, as though it had been written a long while ago, and there was a musty smell about the book which told her it had not been opened for a long while either. Was this because it had fallen to the back of the shelf or because its owner no longer wanted to read it?

She turned a few more pages and several more followed automatically, as if this was where the book had been most frequently opened. A greying card fell to the floor and she picked it up, realising that it was not a card but a photograph. Quickly she turned it over. A young man in slacks and shirt stared up at her. Blaize!—but so much younger than the one she knew that she was astonished. He was smiling directly into the camera, as was the girl who stood beside him. Miranda's hand trembled and she went up to the window to see the picture more clearly. Light fell full upon it and she could almost imagine herself in the shady garden where this picture had been taken. The couple were standing beneath a huge oak tree whose boughs cast a delicate tracery across the forehead of the girl. Blaize was standing so close to her that they could almost have been one, and there was a buoyant air about him that he did not have today. It was this that made him look so much younger, for the style of the girl's dress told her that the picture was not more than five years old. The girl looked to be about Miranda's own age, which meant she would now be in her late twenties.

Miranda leaned against the window ledge. Was this girl the reason why Blaize was still single? She put the photograph face down into the book again. There was only one poem on this page, and she began to read it:

'Some day I shall rise and leave my friends
And seek you again through the world's far ends,
You whom I found so fair,
(Touch of your hands and smell of your hair!),
My only god in the days that were.'

But this unknown girl was still Blaize's god and, from everything he had said, she knew that he had never forgotten the touch of her hands or the smell of her hair. That was why she had felt she was only a stand-in for another woman when he had kissed her last night; a substitute to take the place of his ideal. Again she looked at the picture, ignoring Blaize and staring instead at the complacent face and soft waving hair of the girl beside him. Though the colour had faded it had not destroyed the peaches and cream complexion and golden hair. She was tall too, for her head came above Blaize's shoulder. Miranda closed the book and was moving to the shelf when the door opened and Ann Kerr came in.

Surprise made Miranda halt. Her hand loosened its grip

on the book and the photograph in it fluttered to the floor. She knelt quickly to pick it up, but Ann came forward and held out her hand for it.

'Good lord!' she said, looking at the volume. 'Was it in there all this time?'

Miranda nodded and felt the book taken from her. She watched as Ann glanced at the poem, put the photograph back and slapped the book on the shelf.

'The love of Blaize's life,' she muttered. 'I'm sure you guessed there'd been someone.'

'I had wondered,' Miranda confessed.

'He doesn't talk about her any more. He didn't from the moment she left him.'

'Was she his wife?'

'Heavens, no!' Ann swung round. 'But as good as—in Blaize's eyes. They'd known each other since they were children. Blaize and Rosemary,' she murmured. 'You couldn't think of one name without automatically thinking of the other. When she married someone else, we couldn't believe it.'

Miranda's breath escaped on a long sigh. Rosemary was married to another man. She tried not to let her relief show as she said: 'What happened?'

'She was engaged to Blaize. He was very much a junior director then and working all hours of the day and night to prove himself. Rosemary's parents went on holiday to South Africa and offered to take her with them. The Lothian was in the middle of some important negotiations and Blaize was too busy to spend much time with her. He felt she would be better and happier if she were away for a few months, so she went with her parents. The first day they arrived in Durban they went to the races and met Harry Dorsen. A week later they were married. I think it was the suddenness of it that shattered Blaize—the fact that she could stop loving him so quickly.'

Miranda pondered on the name Dorsen. 'Doesn't he own some goldmines?' As Ann nodded, other things came to mind. 'I remember reading an article about him. He isn't very young.'

'He was fifty. It was knowing how old he was that forced Blaize to see the sort of girl Rosemary was.' Ann shook her head. 'At least it *should* have forced him. The trouble is that I don't think he's ever accepted it. He's closed his mind to the facts. Since the day he received her telegram— she didn't even have the decency to write or call him—he's never mentioned her name. If he had I would have been much happier, as it is I'm always afraid that one day she'll come back into his life and turn it upside-down again.'

'But she's married,' Miranda pointed out.

'A little thing like a husband wouldn't stop Rosemary from doing what she wanted. And if she wanted Blaize. . . .'

'Your brother is far too logical and astute to be taken in.'

'He's only logical in business. In his personal life he's a fearful idealist and romantic. It's an awful combination.'

'I know.' Miranda sighed, feeling that Ann's description could equally well apply to herself.

'That's why he's never got married,' Ann said. 'You can't imagine the number of girls who've made a play for him. I mean, it's natural, isn't it; he's got everything.'

'Everything,' Miranda echoed, and went to the door. 'Let's have a cup of tea.'

'With some cake. Thinking of Rosemary always leaves a nasty taste in my mouth.'

Together they went to the kitchen and when tea was prepared, Miranda wheeled it into the main living room.

'Were they really childhood sweethearts?' she asked, following her own train of thought.

Ann knew at once to whom she was referring. 'She was the girl next door. Well, a mile away. We had a fair amount of acreage around us. Our father was a farmer.'

'A farmer!'

'Of the tweedy kind. He inherited some money from his father and thought farming was a pleasant way of passing the time. It was only when he died and Blaize took it over that it started to show a real profit. He always had an aptitude for making money. At Eton he would come home at the end of term with more money than he'd been sent away with.' Ann smiled reminiscently. 'He ran a swop shop for comics!'

Miranda laughed. 'I can't imagine it.'

'It's true. Even at Oxford he dabbled in the Stock Market and made money. He joined the Lothian as soon as he came down and after a year he became personal assistant to the owner.'

'It's odd to think of anyone actually owning a bank.'

'Blaize does now,' Ann replied. 'When Lord Lothian retired, he bought him out. My brother is highly eligible. Rosemary must often kick herself for not waiting for him.'

Miranda's ears pricked up at this additional piece of information. 'You mean she left him because he wasn't rich enough for her?'

'What else? Rosemary didn't know the meaning of love. She wanted Blaize because he was the best looking boy in the district and the most important. But very unimportant when compared with Harry Dorsen.'

'Do you think she knows that Blaize is so successful?'

'I'm sure her parents have written and told her. They still live in the village where we were born. I think that's one of the reasons Blaize left it once he started making real money.'

'He's paid a high price for his success,' Miranda said, and saw Ann give her such a speculative look that she hastily proffered more cake and fresh tea.

When Ann left, Miranda succumbed to the temptation of

looking again at the photograph of Blaize and Rosemary. It was a mortifying act, like putting on a hair shirt, and she quickly slipped it back and put it on the shelf. What a fool Blaize was to let his life be spoiled by someone so unworthy of him! It signified a weakness of character that went ill with her earlier assessment of him.

On Wednesday Mrs. Linton telephoned to say Mr. Jefferson had gone to Paris for a couple of days and that if she wanted to return to London until Friday, she could do so.

'It isn't worth it,' said Miranda. 'I'll go into Brighton for the day instead.'

The following morning she did so, and spent several happy hours exploring the cobbled lanes and shops in the old part of the town. There were many antique ones, but they seemed to cater for tourists and although some of the things were good, they were expensive, while the cheap things were merely junk. To cheer herself up she bought a couple of dresses instead and debated which one to wear during the coming weekend. It was dusk when she drove back, having borrowed one of the small cars from the garage, and she experienced a sense of homecoming as she bowled along the drive and saw the house in front of her, its windows glinting in the darkness. How easy it would be to make this her permanent home! It was a dangerous thought and she shied away from it. But it was impossible not to wonder how her relationship with Blaize would progress during the coming weekend. He had said he would not kiss her again and she knew he meant it. But if she showed him that she wanted him to do so.... These thoughts were dangerous too, and she concentrated on putting the car in the garage and locking the doors.

The staff greeted her like a long-lost friend and she had to display her purchases to Maria and Iñez, who exclaimed in delight at her appearance and chatted happily over her head in Spanish. This had been her happiest day here so far, and that night she slept dreamlessly and awoke late to find the sun streaming through the open casement window. In a demure housecoat she went downstairs to have breakfast and decided to have it sitting on the lawn. Sipping her fragrant coffee, she looked dreamily out on to the rolling landscape. The telephone pealed in the distance and José came to tell her that Mrs. Kerr was on the line.

'What sort of salad shall I make her for lunch?' Miranda mused as she went to take the call. But Ann was not thinking of lunch: she had far more disturbing news to impart.

'Harry Dorsen was killed in a car crash a week ago,' she said. 'The news has only just been released and Mark called me from London to tell me.'

Miranda did not know what to say. Ann's words raised a whole host of imponderables, all of them uninviting. 'Does your brother know?' she asked.

'Of course. It's splashed all over the City pages. It means Rosemary is free, of course. I always knew she would be one day, but I was hoping Blaize would be married by then. Now there's nothing to stop him running to her.'

'Even if he'd been married,' Miranda retorted, 'it would take more than a wife to hold him back, if he's as obsessed by her as that.'

A heavy sigh came through the receiver. 'Well, he isn't married, and there's no point talking about it. I only wanted to tell you the news in case he says anything when he comes down this weekend.'

'He isn't likely to talk to me about her,' said Miranda. 'I'm only the cook.'

When she put down the receiver the pleasure had gone from the day, and she took her tray back to the kitchen and then wandered round the house like a ghost. With despairing eyes she looked at each room, savouring its charm and trying not to see a tall fair-haired girl as mistress here.

There had been no word from Mrs. Linton to say what

time Blaize would be arriving, nor any mention of guests, and she called the woman herself to find out.

'I was waiting until the last moment before telephoning you,' Mrs. Linton explained, 'just in case Mr. Jefferson didn't get back from Paris. But he walked in half an hour ago and he won't be bringing anyone down with him. He's had a difficult week and I think he's looking forward to a rest.'

Miranda would have liked to know whether his difficulties had been business or personal—Rosemary's reappearance, possibly—but Mrs. Linton rang off before she could find a subtle way of phrasing the question, which was all to the good, she thought as she returned to the kitchen to plan the meals for the weekend. She wanted to have as much spare time as possible in case Blaize wanted her to stay with him, and to this end she concentrated on casseroles and soups that could be prepared in advance, with several luscious sweets to satisfy his sweet tooth. At six o'clock she was dressed for his arrival, her palms tingling with excitement each time she heard a car in the distance. But it always remained distant and it was nine o'clock before he finally arrived, pale and tired, with bruised shadows beneath his eyes. She hovered in the background as José took his briefcase and coat, then came forward tentatively to ask if he wanted to eat now or later.

'I've already dined,' he said abruptly, and strode into the library. No sooner had he closed the door than he opened it and called her name.

She was by the servants' door and she stopped and looked at him.

'I've had a hell of a day, Miranda, forgive me.'

'Of course.'

'I'll have some coffee,' he said, speaking again. 'Tell José to bring it up to my bedroom.'

There could have been no quicker way of wishing her

goodnight, and hurt by the rebuff she returned to the kitchen. Sleep did not come easily that night and she read for a long time, eventually putting the book aside to lean out of the window and look at the garden. There was a full moon and the paths were clearly visible. The tall figure of a man was slowly moving along one of them and she recognised Blaize. She knew without being told that he too found it impossible to sleep, and wished with all her heart that she did not know the reason for it. But it was all too obvious. The weariness on his face, apart from his abrupt manner towards her, made that abundantly clear.

In the morning, heavy-eyed and listless, she prepared the lunch and then deliberately remained in the kitchen. If Blaize wanted to see her he would have to single her out. At eleven o'clock when José returned from taking him his morning coffee, he told her Mrs. Kerr and her husband would be coming to lunch.

They arrived at midday, bringing Mark junior with them and Ann brought him into the kitchen to show him off. He was a chubby, placid baby sleeping peacefully in his mother's arms and not bothering to wake up to receive the admiration bestowed on him.

'You'll be lunching with us, won't you?' Ann asked, as she went to put the baby back in his pram.

'No, I won't,' Miranda replied, 'and please don't suggest it to your brother. You'll embarrass me if you do.'

'That's ridiculous!' said Ann.

'I don't see why. Mrs. Holden didn't eat with you.'

Ann opened her mouth and then shut it again, but it had been obvious what she had been about to say and Miranda warmed to her.

'I would sooner eat with the staff,' she continued quietly.

'When will I see you, then? You're leaving on Monday, aren't you?'

'Yes, but I'm sure we'll meet again one day.'

It was only when lunch had been served and cleared away that the parlourmaid came in and said that Mr. Jefferson had asked her to take coffee with them. Miranda's instinct was to refuse, but she forced herself not to do so, intent on showing him she did not care whether or not she saw him. But entering the sitting room she was glad he could not hear her heart hammering or know how weak her knees went at the sight of him. He looked more rested today, though the shadows were still in his eyes, and he patted the seat beside him. She sat down and gave him a bright smile.

'You should have joined us for lunch,' he said.

'You should have asked me.'

'I didn't know you were waiting for an invitation.'

'I can't just sit myself at your table,' she protested.

'I refuse to believe you're shy.'

'I know my place,' she said primly.

Ann heard the last sentence. 'You should wear a black dress and white apron when you say that!'

'Miranda was deliberately being provocative,' Blaize informed the room at large. 'Take no notice of her.'

'I hear you're going back to London on Monday,' Mark Kerr said to her. 'I'll give you a lift if you like.'

'What's wrong with my car?' Blaize said before Miranda could reply, and his response made her feel that perhaps she had misjudged his behaviour last night. It could have stemmed from genuine tiredness and not from regret at having established an intimacy with her last weekend. Certainly his asking her to have coffee with him this afternoon showed his wish to be friendly.

'I'd better take the baby back,' said Mark, standing up. 'I promised Nanny I'd return him by three.' He looked at his wife. 'What time shall I come back for you, darling?'

'There's no need. I'll walk back.'

'A good idea. If you don't use your legs a bit more my

96

second child will be born with wheels!' With a cheerful wave he went out, and Ann stood up and watched through the window as he and the pram disappeared round the bend in the drive.

'It does my female heart good to see a man pushing a pram,' she commented. 'Oh dear, the baby's dropped a toy on the path.'

'I'll run after him and give it to him,' Miranda jumped up and ran through the French windows. She was not sure why she had taken this chance of escaping, she only knew that she found it difficult to sit close to Blaize. When she came back she would take one of the armchairs. She picked up the woolly rabbit and hurried after Mark, pausing again to admire the baby, who was now awake and staring at her with an intense expression.

'He really looks as if he knows what's going on,' she chuckled. 'I'd love to have a baby like him.'

'I don't think Ann would let me oblige,' Mark teased. 'But if you can persuade her....'

Laughing, Miranda strolled back to the house. As she reached the windows she heard Ann's voice, high and angry.

'Honestly, Blaize, you're out of your mind! You should have refused to take the call.'

'What good would that have done?' He sounded angry too. 'I can't forget the past.'

'You could if you made a present for yourself—or even tried to think in terms of a future.'

Miranda hesitated, unwilling to enter the room in the middle of a family quarrel. She backed away, inadvertently knocking against one of the garden chairs. Biting her lip, she backed away further.

'For heaven's sake come in!' Blaize called. 'Your flapping ears are causing a draught.'

Embarrassed, Miranda stepped into the room. 'I would

have to be deaf not to hear the two of you.'

'You don't have to listen.'

'Blaize!' Ann cried. 'Don't be so rude.'

Blaize's jaw clenched. 'Miranda doesn't need you to defend her.' He gave Miranda a haughty stare. 'Sit down and stop looking so hurt.'

'Blaize!' Ann said again, but he merely gave an irritable exclamation and sunk his head lower on his shoulders.

'What did she say when she called you?' Ann was speaking to her brother again.

'You'll only get more annoyed if I tell you.'

'I couldn't get *more* annoyed. So for goodness' sake tell me what she wanted. I must say she has a nerve. Her husband isn't cold in his grave yet.'

'They weren't living together,' Blaize muttered. 'They were getting divorced.'

'You mean darling Rosemary had made a terrible mistake?'

'As a matter of fact she did,' her brother said coldly. 'It might be difficult for you, cocooned in a happy marriage— to know that some men can turn out to be swines.'

'Or can wake up to the truth! Perhaps Harry Dorsen wasn't as stupid as you.'

'Ann!' Blaize stormed. 'If you can't talk about Rosemary sensibly, then don't talk about her at all.'

'Suits me,' Ann said promptly.

Miranda could not bear to listen to this conversation, and jumping to her feet she ran across the room. It was unfortunate that just at this moment Blaize should decide that he too had had enough. Whirling round to go into the garden, he collided with Miranda and sent her spinning to the floor. The breath was knocked from her body and she lay there, winded.

Instantly Blaize bent over her, his expression anxious.

'Miranda! Are you hurt?'

She shook her head and felt herself being gently lifted to her feet and held there. For the first time this weekend hazel eyes stared at her with tenderness and she wanted to wallow in the look. But all too soon it became distant again and his arms dropped to his sides.

'You're still a jinx,' he said softly, and went out into the garden.

The two girls looked at each other. 'I suppose you know what we were arguing about?' Ann said.

'I gather Rosemary called him from Africa.'

'Too right. Playing the bereaved widow, though from what she told Blaize, she'd been hoping to become a gay divorcee. If one can believe her, that is. Knowing Rosemary, she probably made up the whole story.'

'Why?'

'Because then she'd have no reason to wait before making a set at Blaize.'

There was the throaty noise of an old engine and Ann's head tilted. 'That's the village taxi. I wonder who it is?'

She went into the hall and Miranda followed, watching as Ann opened the front door and then fell back a step. 'Oh, lord,' Ann muttered. 'It's happening just the way I knew it would!'

A car door slammed and light steps heralded the appearance of a tall, slender woman, her fairness enhanced by a beige silk suit.

'Ann dear, how nice to see you after all these years. You haven't changed a bit.'

'You have,' said Ann. 'You look older.'

'And wiser,' came the reply, as the woman stepped further into the hall. Instantly she saw Miranda and for split second she paused. Then she glanced at Ann. 'I know Blaize isn't married. I spoke to him on Wednesday.'

'Miranda is a friend of ours,' Ann said coldly, and looked at Miranda beseechingly. 'This is Rosemary Dorsen, an ex-girl-friend of Blaize's.'

'You really haven't changed,' Rosemary said to Ann. 'You're as rude as ever.'

'Ruder,' Ann retorted. 'Why have you come back? What do you want?'

'Blaize,' said Rosemary, 'and I'm going to have him.'

Miranda felt sickened. Was this the girl Blaize had loved for so long, this beautiful arrogant creature, recently widowed yet standing there in finery that made her look like a radiant bride?

'I was planning to come back anyway,' Rosemary continued. 'Harry's death merely precipitated it by a few weeks.'

'Blaize doesn't want you,' Ann said haughtily.

Rosemary laughed, a tinkling sound that died away as heavy steps came across the sitting room floor. Miranda, still standing by the threshold, knew Blaize was directly behind her. She heard his sharp intake of breath, then he murmured Rosemary's name, making it sound almost like a benediction and giving away so much of his feelings that Miranda wanted to cry. Though the woman could not have heard him speak she knew immediately that he was there, and she came towards him, her hands outstretched, her china blue eyes glittering with tears.

'Blaize,' she said huskily. 'How wonderful to see you again!'

Miranda knew she should move out of the way, but some perverse streak made her stay where she was. Her presence made it impossible for Blaize to rush forward, and he flung her a look, almost as if he guessed that this was her intention.

'Hello, Rosemary,' he said carefully.

Hearing him speak, Miranda could not credit that it was the same voice that had uttered the girl's name a few seconds ago, for it was now cool and controlled.

'You should have warned me that you were coming,' he continued.

'I didn't know myself until this morning. I flew into London late last night and telephoned your home, but they said you were here. So I decided to come down and surprise you.' She glanced beyond Blaize. 'Aren't you going to invite me in?'

'Of course.' He stepped back and Rosemary followed him.

Ann hurried after them, attempting to pull Miranda in with her. But Miranda had had enough, and with a shake of her head she ran down the hall to the kitchen. What a fool she had been ever to leave it!

CHAPTER SEVEN

BANGING saucepans was an excellent way of giving vent to one's temper, Miranda found, though the clatter brought José scurrying in to ask if anything was wrong.

'Everything is fine,' she said brightly, 'but I think there'll be an extra guest for dinner.'

As she spoke the bell rang from the drawing room and he went to answer it. When he returned it was to call his wife Maria. Miranda, though only partly able to follow the rapid conversation, realised that Rosemary would be staying as a weekend guest. From what Ann had told her of Rosemary's behaviour she had hoped that a man of Blaize's strength of character would not allow himself to be used again. But men, it seemed, could be as tender-hearted as women when chivalry was called into play, and there was nothing more guaranteed to bring this out than golden hair, baby blue eyes and a husky voice with a faint lisp to it.

Forcing herself to give Rosemary the benefit of the

doubt—after all, Ann could be prejudiced and there might be extenuating circumstances to the other girl's behaviour—Miranda re-examined the dinner menu and decided to make a more elaborate hors d'oeuvres. There were mushrooms in the larder and she set these to sauté lightly while she took a carton of stock and some cream from the deep freeze. What a boon a freezer was when it was carefully filled, and how much better use she would make of it than Mrs. Holden, who appeared to use it mainly for keeping game and blanched vegetables. She set the stock to simmer and was stirring it when Blaize came into the kitchen. His face was marred by a scowl and though it made him look irritable it also made him look younger.

'What do you want?' she asked abruptly.

He stopped short, taken aback by her tone. It made her remember that he was her employer and though she could not bring herself to apologise for her tone, she tried to look conciliatory.

'I'm sorry to disturb you while you're in the middle of cooking.' Blaize was evidently prepared to accept the rumour that most cooks were bad-tempered when caught in their kitchen. 'I wanted to make sure you know that I expect you to dine with us.'

'Why should you expect it?' she said, concentrating on the pan as though she had never seen one before.

'You had supper with me last Sunday, didn't you?'

'You were alone last Sunday.'

'That's beside the point. Look, don't argue about it. We have already had this out and I told you I saw no reason for you to eat in the kitchen.'

'I prefer to be treated as your staff,' said Miranda. 'I'm not a friend of yours.'

'What's got into you?' It was the standard male cry for any feminine remark they did not understand, and he looked so disconcerted that she was contrite.

102

'Nothing has got into me, Blaize. It's just that I don't want to be in the way, and you do have another visitor.'

'It's because I do that I ... Let's not discuss it any more,' he continued abruptly. 'I want you to dine with me tonight and for the rest of the weekend.'

'What would happen if I refused?'

'You will not refuse,' he said coldly, and despite his informal clothes he was every inch the man in control of the situation.

She reacted to it instinctively by nodding agreement, but later in her own room, changing before going downstairs to join him, she was annoyed that she had succumbed so easily to his order. After all, he had engaged her as a temporary cook, not a stand-in guest. Though she did not want to dwell on his reason for asking her to join him, it was impossible not to do so. He was obviously afraid that if he were alone with Rosemary he would fall under her spell again. Though she was astonished by his weakness it was Rosemary's behaviour that astonished her more. How thick-skinned she was to come chasing after Blaize when she had only been widowed two weeks! Of course she had said she had already left her husband, but somehow Miranda doubted this. One thing she did know, however: Rosemary had not loved the recently killed Harry, nor did she love Blaize. She was a woman who only loved herself.

Miranda had vowed not to dress up tonight, but her decision had been short-lived and she put on the dress she had bought in Brighton. It was black and simple in the extreme, relying for its effect on the starkness of its colour against her creamy skin and the sinuous moulding of its material to every line of her body. It was impossible for her to wear anything underneath it, and this was apparent to any appraising eye. It was not the dress to wear to a church social, but was definitely the right choice if one wanted to show a beautiful widow that she was not going to have everything her own way.

Miranda applied more make-up than usual, lengthening and darkening eyelashes that did not require this extra artifice, deliberately exaggerating the tilt of her eyes with fine black eye-liner and drawing attention to her wide, beautifully-shaped mouth by a pale glistening lipstick. She kept her hair style as simple as her dress, and it fell long and silky smooth to her shoulders, the ends curling softly. So must Cleopatra have looked when she had gone to seduce Antony. It was a fanciful thought, but it remained with Miranda as she went slowly down to the sitting room.

One look at Rosemary's face told Miranda that the girl had not known she would be dining with them. The rose-petal mouth tightened and for an instant the soft blue eyes went hard, but she recovered her equilibrium and gave her a bright smile, though she did not include Miranda in the conversation and went on talking to Blaize as though they were alone.

'Harry's death was a tragedy, of course, but I always thought he would come to a violent end. He should never have driven a car when he was in one of his rages. It stopped him from thinking clearly.'

'As you weren't living with him,' Blaize commented, 'you can't blame yourself for his last rage.'

Rosemary sighed. 'I have enough on my conscience anyway.'

'You mustn't go on blaming yourself for the past,' Blaize said. 'The thing is to recognise one's mistakes and then go on from there.'

'You make it sound so easy.' Rosemary leaned towards him as if trying to exclude Miranda completely. 'But you can't forget the past unless you know that the person you've wronged has forgiven you.'

Miranda waited tensely for Blaize's reply, but he allowed his expression to speak for him, and since he was half turned

104

away from her she could only see the momentary tilt of his head. How handsome he was, she thought illogically. The nervous vitality he exuded added to his sensuous attraction. One sensed his tightly leashed passion, the icy control he was putting on himself, and she knew there was not a woman in the world who would not feel the urge to break it down.

'Would either of you like another drink?' she asked brightly. 'I can get it while I pour one for myself.'

Blaize flushed and took the hint. 'Sorry,' he said jerkily, and went to the sideboard where a bottle of champagne was on ice.

Miranda wondered drearily what he was celebrating. 'No champagne for me,' she said aloud. 'It gives me hiccups.'

Rosemary laughed. 'For the first time you sound as young as you look.'

'I'm twenty-two,' Miranda said, and wished she could say something cutting about Rosemary's age. But the girl looked little older than herself, though she was nearer thirty. Tonight she looked lovely enough to disturb any man's peace of mind, ethereal in floating violet chiffon. She was without a doubt a chocolate box blonde, and Miranda would have taken a bet that her wardrobe held no colour more dramatic than rose pink.

'I'll have some more champagne, darling,' Rosemary said, and held out her glass for Blaize to replenish with his own.

He did so, and went to sit in an armchair, leaving Rosemary and Miranda together on a settee. Miranda felt the two of them must make a stark contrast, one dark as night, the other fair as day, and knew bleakly she did not have to wonder which type Blaize preferred.

'I understand you do the cooking here.' Rosemary was speaking to her and Miranda forced herself to pay attention.

'Only while Mrs. Holden is away.'

'You still have Mrs. Holden?' Rosemary said to Blaize. He nodded. 'Nothing has changed.'

'I hope you mean that,' she whispered back, her voice so breathless that Miranda controlled an urge to blow a raspberry. What an act the girl was putting on, simpering at Blaize like a schoolgirl when she already had one husband behind her and another one on whom she had set her sights.

Draining her glass, Miranda stood up. 'Excuse me for a moment while I pop into the kitchen and see that everything is ready.'

'Don't ask me to help you,' Rosemary cooed, 'I'm absolutely hopeless in the kitchen.'

But wonderful in the bedroom, no doubt, Miranda thought crossly as she went out. As she made sure the mushroom vol-au-vents were hot enough, she told herself not to read animosity into Rosemary's attitude to her. There was time enough to do so if she became convinced the girl was being deliberately antagonistic.

She did not have to wait long to form a judgment on this point, for during dinner Rosemary ignored her completely, only including her in the conversation to make a comment on the food, thus firmly reinstating Miranda in her position as cook.

If Blaize noticed, he gave no sign of it, seemingly content to let Rosemary control the conversation. Tired of being ignored, Miranda asked the most provocative questions she could.

'When are you going back to Africa, Mrs. Dorsen?'

China blue eyes widened, but the face remained innocent. 'I'm not sure. I have no personal reason to return there. All my family are here and I made no close friends during my marriage.' The blonde head turned to Blaize. 'Harry never kept his friends for long—except the ones who worked for him.'

'He must have had something nice about him,' Miranda said artlessly, 'or you wouldn't have married him.'

This time the blue eyes showed a distinct iciness, though the voice remained soft. 'I was young and foolish when I married Harry. He was strong and he bowled me over.'

'Money has a habit of doing that,' Miranda said.

Blaize set his glass down sharply. 'Are you going to live with your parents, Rosemary?' he asked.

'Oh no, I want a home of my own. I was hoping perhaps you could advise me.'

'You've always had a mind of your own,' he said, smiling slightly.

'And look what trouble it's caused me.' She threw out her hands. 'I'm afraid I've lost confidence in my own judgment. From now on I want to be told what to do. I was thinking of moving into a furnished flat in London until I've decided.'

'Property is extremely expensive these days.'

'Money is no problem,' Rosemary smiled. 'That's one nice thing I *can* say about Harry. He was always generous.' She leaned towards Blaize. 'It's so wonderful to know that from now on I need only be guided by my heart.'

'Haven't you always been guided by your heart?' Miranda inquired guilelessly.

'Unfortunately not. I allowed Harry's wealth to sway me. You were right about that.'

Miranda lowered her eyes, surprised by the admission until she realised how clever it was. For Rosemary to maintain she had married Harry Dorsen for love would nullify her assertion that she had always been in love with Blaize. She obviously considered it better to admit that money had made her forget love rather than that there had been no love there in the first place.

'To understand what I did,' Rosemary was speaking

again, 'you would have to know my background. Blaize always had enough money and because of it he can't see why it was so important to me.'

'It was important because you made it so,' he said.

'*I* didn't make it so,' Rosemary protested, and looked at Miranda again. 'My father was an army officer and my mother came from a very rich family who lost all their wealth. I was her only child and I was pretty enough to make them think I could retrieve the family fortunes.'

'It sounds like a plot in a novelette,' Miranda said.

'Probably my mother read it too.' It was the first humorous remark Rosemary had made, but Miranda was convinced the story was untrue.

'You mean your parents pushed you into your marriage?'

'In a way.'

'Do you really need to rake over the ashes?' Blaize cut in.

'I don't mind Miranda asking questions,' said Rosemary. 'It's much better to clear the air than to have the feeling that the questions Miranda is asking are in your mind too.'

'I don't know why you say that,' he said stiffly. 'I told you earlier that the past is finished.'

'Your eyes belied your words,' Rosemary whispered.

'I'm still here,' Miranda said in a clear voice, 'but I can leave if I'm in the way.'

'You could never be in the way,' Blaize said silkily. 'We mustn't let Rosemary monopolise the conversation. It's a tendency she had even as a child!'

'And you always teased me about it,' Rosemary chuckled. 'You haven't changed a bit.'

'I don't think people do change. They merely learn to simulate more.'

'I'm not pretending,' Rosemary whispered. 'For the first time in my life I can do what I want.'

Miranda felt the tension between the man and the

woman and knew that Blaize was fighting against it, trying not to let himself be drawn into a vortex that could end only with his capitulation.

'What exactly do you want, Mrs. Dorsen?' Miranda heard herself ask, and saw Rosemary fling her a look of positive dislike.

'Love,' came the reply. 'The love that I was too foolish to recognise when I was your age.'

'What makes you think you can recognise it now?' Blaize asked, his voice expressionless.

'I don't *think*,' Rosemary said passionately. 'I know! And so do you.' The blue eyes flashed at Miranda as if willing her to get up and leave. 'Oh, darling,' Rosemary said huskily, and put her hand to her eyes. 'There were so many times when I would have given anything in the world to have been able to talk to you, to ask your help ... only I didn't have the right until I was free.'

Miranda listened with disbelief. What gall Rosemary had to talk like this, yet from the look on Blaize's face, he believed every word. He was a fool, and she couldn't stay here and watch him. She pushed back her chair and the sound made Blaize turn to her.

'Where are you going, Miranda?'

'I'm sure you and Mrs. Dorsen don't need me as an audience. If you want me to clap at the final scene you'll find me in the kitchen.'

'What final scene?' he demanded.

'The capitulation. Or perhaps I should say recapitulation?'

His eyes glittered and she was delighted to see it. It meant his temper was returning and with it, she hoped, some of his backbone. If only he would put up some fight against Rosemary instead of acting like a jellyfish!

'Sit down, Miranda,' he said abruptly.

'I can understand how Miranda feels,' Rosemary murmured. 'She doesn't know about us and——'

'But I do,' said Miranda. 'Everybody knows you jilted Blaize for a rich old man!'

Rosemary's sharply drawn breath told Miranda she had finally succeeded in discomfiting the girl. But she was not quite sure if this was a victory, for Blaize's eyes were upon her like pinpoints of ice. But it was Rosemary who spoke, her voice thick with emotion.

'If one hears the story second-hand it does sound rather callous, but there were circumstances I couldn't fight. If you love your parents they can put a pressure on you that's hard to resist.'

Miranda glanced at Blaize, wondering how much longer *he* would be able to resist, and fearing from the look on his face that his downfall was imminent. He was so pale that his hair was like jet. It had the shine of jet too, and she longed to touch the silky strands the way she had touched them last week. She looked at Rosemary's hands, knowing bleakly that it was those plump little fingers that would be caressing Blaize from now on. If only she had never agreed to have dinner here! If only she had never come to the house in the first place.

'I do think you should let Miranda go if she wishes,' Rosemary said to Blaize. 'I know how she feels.'

'I'm not sure you do.' He reached out across the table and found Miranda's hand on her lap. His own was ice cold, the fingers trembling slightly, though his voice was composed as he went on: 'I don't think we should hide the truth from Rosemary any longer, darling. I know your passion for secrecy, but——' He pulled Miranda's hand above the table and went on pulling it until it was against his lips. His eyes were half hidden by lowered lids as though he could not bear anyone to stare directly into them.

Miranda did not know what he was talking about, nor did Rosemary, it seemed, for she gave him an odd look as

110

she spoke.

'What truth are you talking about, Blaize?'

'About Miranda and myself.' He was on his feet and he came to stand behind Miranda's chair. He dropped her hand, but only to place both of his on her shoulders. They were hard on the nape of her neck, almost as if he was ready to choke her if she did not do as he said.

'Miranda and I are engaged. I suppose it's fitting that you should be the first to know.'

Miranda swallowed hard and, feeling her convulsive movement, the fingers tightened more. The pain of his hold acted as a brake, making it impossible for her to cry out, but not so Rosemary, whose gasp of shock was audible and whose look was anything but felicitous.

'Did you say you and Miranda are *engaged*?'

'Secretly—until this moment.' Blaize swooped down till his cheek rested against Miranda's. His breath was fast and warm on her skin, and swivelling her head she saw the shine of sweat on his upper lip. Her instinctive reaction to deny what he had just said died as she saw this visible sign of his distress and, as always, the tenderness he could arouse in her was her undoing. He was using her because he needed her, and though she disliked him for it, she could not let him down.

'And they say a woman can't keep a secret!' she snorted. 'Honestly, Blaize!' With an effort she smiled at Rosemary. 'But I suppose it was better to tell you the truth than have you think he was still free.'

Rosemary brought out a wisp of lace handkerchief. 'I should have known nothing lasts for ever. It was foolish of me to think that we....'

Her voice sank away, but Miranda was aware of the effect it had on the man behind her. It was not only his hands that were trembling, but his whole body. If she had wanted a further sign that Rosemary still had power over him, she was getting it now.

'Nothing *does* last for ever, Rosemary,' he said harshly. 'It took me a long time to get over you, but—but then I met Miranda.'

'So different from me,' Rosemary whispered, and put her hand to her hair as if to stress the point.

'So different from you,' Blaize agreed, and let his eyes meet Miranda's aquamarine ones. But his were sightless, as if he were gazing inwards. 'Perhaps it was because Miranda was so different that she appealed to me. It's like Swan Lake, isn't it? The black swan and the white one.'

Since the black swan had not got her man in the end, Miranda could have done without that particular comment. But she was glad Blaize had said something to irritate her, for it lessened her sympathy for him and gave her back her strength of mind. 'Now we've told Rosemary the truth perhaps I'll have some champagne after all.' Green eyes sparkled up at him. 'I'm so glad the truth is out. It makes me see how silly I was to want to keep our engagement a secret.'

'When is the wedding day?' Rosemary asked, in control of herself again.

'In the autumn,' Blaize said before Miranda could reply. 'But she's being coy about that too.'

'It's good for a girl to play hard to get,' said Rosemary. 'I congratulate you, Miranda.'

'*You* don't believe in playing hard to get,' Miranda retorted, and felt Blaize stiffen beside her, as if he did not like her to be rude to the woman he still so obviously wanted.

'If you mean that I've never pretended about the way I feel,' Rosemary said, 'then you're quite right. But when you've made one stupid mistake you realise how unimportant pride is. I'm not going to pretend that your news hasn't been a shock.'

'I'm sure you'll recover,' Blaize said quietly.

112

'Recover whom?' Rosemary asked with a slight smile. 'You aren't married yet, darling.'

'Do you hear that, Blaize?' Miranda twisted round to look into his face. 'Perhaps we'd better set the wedding date after all!' She linked her arm through his and only then did she swing back to look at Rosemary. 'You know the old story about a bird in the hand, and though I haven't got mine in the oven yet he's well and truly plucked and tied!'

It was only when Blaize went to see about bringing up another bottle of champagne from the cellar—José being unable to find the particular vintage required—that Miranda was left alone with Rosemary for the first time since they had met. She braced herself for the attack, not sure what was coming, knowing only that it would be as hurtful as Rosemary could make it.

'You don't think I believe this nonsense about your engagement,' the blonde girl said. 'I know exactly why Blaize is pretending.'

Miranda gave her full marks for conceit. Only such a woman could believe that a man could still love her after the callous way she had behaved towards him. However, she was not prepared to throw in the towel so easily and she gave Rosemary a cool stare. 'Believe what you like, Mrs. Dorsen, but Blaize happens to have told you the truth.'

'Then why didn't he say so this afternoon? I don't believe you wanted to keep it a secret. Any girl lucky enough to get him would want to shout it from the housetops.'

'You didn't. You jilted him for someone else.'

'I was stupid. Anyway, at that time Blaize was not in the position that he is today.'

'We're not all as mercenary as you. I love Blaize—but I wanted to be quite sure before I finally committed myself. I can promise you he didn't make it up.'

113

'He wouldn't allow you to act as his cook if he were going to marry you.'

'I'm only doing what most women do for their husbands,' Miranda said humorously, 'with the exception that I'm actually getting a salary for it! Besides, if I'd come down to stay with him all his friends would have gossiped about it, but as his cook, my presence goes unremarked.'

There was sufficient truth in this statement for Rosemary to be uncertain whether or not it was a lie, but before she could return to the attack Blaize came back. Champagne was opened and Miranda, seeing the glint in his eye, was prepared for the toast he made.

'To you and our future, my darling Miranda. May it always be as effervescent as the champagne.'

'With all our bubbles little ones!' she quipped.

He chuckled, the first sign of humour he had shown since Rosemary had arrived in his home. 'Never short of an answer, are you?' he said softly.

'Nor are you,' she said equally softly, then, aware of Rosemary watching, perched herself on the arm of his chair.

The conversation for the next hour was stilted and only became animated when Rosemary started to discuss her late husband's business interests. His death had come before their divorce had reached any stage of finality, she said, but she was so vague about it that Miranda was more certain than ever that there had been no divorce pending, and that Rosemary had made it up in order to account for her complete lack of mourning and her immediate return to London. This alone could account for Harry Dorsen leaving her his entire fortune, which was considerable and which she wanted Blaize to look after.

'There's no one I trust more than you,' she murmured. 'I hope Miranda won't be jealous if I ask you to take care of my affairs.'

'As long as they're only financial ones,' Miranda quipped.

'Don't you think it might be better for you to go to someone else?' said Blaize, ignoring the interruption.

'Not unless you insist. There'll be a large amount of money to invest, and I have total faith in you. Anyway, doesn't the bank want wealthy clients?'

'Of course we do.'

'Then why are you turning me down? Is it because you no longer love me?'

Blaize was so motionless he could have been carved from stone and several seconds passed before he answered. 'When you put it like that you make it difficult for me to say no.'

'Then it's settled.' Rosemary's skirts fanned around her as she rose. 'Do forgive me if I go to bed. The excitement of seeing you again has made me tired.'

'I'll show you to your room,' he said, and walked towards the door. 'Are you going to bed too, Miranda?' he asked over his shoulders.

'Not yet, darling,' Miranda trilled and, from the colour that came into Rosemary's peachy skin, knew the girl had planned to keep him with her.

Had they been lovers in the past? It was a question that had been in her mind since she had discovered the snapshot. Now it was a conscious thought and refused to be ignored. Moral standards were laxer today than five years ago, but even at that time many engaged couples had anticipated marriage. If Rosemary and Blaize had done so, she would not put it past the girl to be willing to do so again and, from the fatuous look on Blaize's face, it would be all too easy.

Ostentatiously she curled herself more closely into the corner of the settee. 'I'll wait here for you, darling. Be as quick as you can.'

CHAPTER EIGHT

ALONE in the room Miranda looked with displeasure at her glass of champagne. It was as flat as the evening had gone, though her temper rose the more she pondered on its events. How overpowering of Blaize to use her as a protection against Rosemary, and how typical to assume that she would fall in with his wishes! Would she have let herself become enveigled into this position if she had not been in love with him, and was it because he knew how she felt that he had used her? This thought was more horrifying than anything else. The last thing in the world she wanted was for Blaize to know the truth. Agitatedly she paced the floor. Yesterday, this morning even, she would not have cared if he had discovered it, but now that she knew he still loved Rosemary she would do everything in her power to prevent him knowing what her own feelings were for him. The door clicked and the object of her bitter thoughts stood in front of her.

'I'm glad you waited for me, Miranda. I wanted to talk to you.'

'Let me try and guess why,' she said sardonically. 'Don't tell me you want to call off our engagement already?'

'No,' he said quickly. 'I hope you'll bear with me over that. But I want to explain why I did it. I hadn't planned it, you know, but seeing you and Rosemary arguing——'

'Correction,' Miranda interrupted. 'Your lady love was being rude to *me*—not the other way around.'

'You gave as good as you got,' he said shortly, and made a disclaiming gesture, as if it did not matter any more. 'Rosemary was obviously put out at having you dine with us, and that gave me the idea of getting engaged to you.'

'For how long?' she demanded sweetly. 'I assume you don't intend to see it through to the end.'

'The end?'

'Marriage,' she explained. 'You aren't suggesting we get married in order to prove to Rosemary that you can live without her?'

His discomfiture was apparent. 'I hadn't thought that far ahead,' he said stiffly. 'If you could bear with me for the next month or so—until Rosemary has settled in London and made another life for herself. . . .'

'You mean until she finds another man? Honestly, Blaize, haven't you any guts? Do you have to hide behind one woman in order to escape from another?'

'When you put it like that you make me sound a complete fool,' he said jerkily.

'You *are* a complete fool! You despise Rosemary for the way she behaved, but you're still scared that you'll fall for her all over again! And now you're using me as a barricade. You're more than a fool, Blaize, you're a coward!'

'You don't mince your words, do you? But then you never have with me. I suppose that's one of the reasons why I trust you.'

'You don't know me well enough to trust me,' she said crossly, and turned her back on him. 'Anyway, the whole thing is a waste of time. Rosemary knows our engagement is a farce. She told me so.'

'I don't believe you.' He came over and pulled her round to face him. 'You're making it up because you don't want to help me.'

'Why shouldn't I want to help you? I'm a great one for lost causes!' She jerked free of him. 'When you went out to get the champagne, Rosemary said you were still in love with her and were using me as a buffer. I must say I give her full marks for being bright.'

Blaize swore softly under his breath, though sufficient

117

words were audible to bring the colour to Miranda's cheeks, a fact which he noticed immediately. 'Forgive me,' he said contritely, and suddenly sat down in a chair as if he no longer had the strength to stand. 'I don't blame you for despising me. You've obviously never been in love yourself—never been hurt—and you can't understand how I felt when Rosemary left me. I vowed I would never let myself go through the same experience.'

'You can only be sure of that by never falling in love.'

'That's it exactly! That's why I'm determined not to let Rosemary into my life again.' He leaned forward. 'Play along with me, Miranda. Rosemary may say she doesn't believe us, but I'm sure she isn't as positive as she pretends.'

Miranda hesitated. 'It wasn't fair of you to put me in this position without asking me first.'

'Would you have refused?'

'Yes.'

'That's why I didn't ask you! Dash it all, why can't you help me out?' He paused, as if a thought had suddenly struck him. 'You aren't engaged to anyone else, are you?'

'No.'

'Then pretend you're engaged to me. I'll make it worth your while.'

It was the last thing she had expected to hear and she was speechless with temper. It had been sufficiently lowering to her pride to have him think he could call on her help without a 'by your leave', but for him to offer to pay her for it was turning an act of help into a service!

'I have said the wrong thing, haven't I?' Blaize spoke again and was on his feet and coming towards her. 'I'm sorry, Miranda, I must be catching your habit of being tactless.'

'I'm not tactless, Blaize; I'm truthful.'

'I've been truthful with you, too. I need your help,

Miranda.'

'It's a good thing your board of directors can't see you now,' she taunted, and saw the colour come into his face. Many other jibes lay on the tip of her tongue, but she held them back, afraid that if she uttered them he might guess her anger stemmed from jealousy. 'Very well,' she said abruptly. 'I'll do as you want. But you'd better brush up on your acting if you want Rosemary to think you're in love with me.'

'Men aren't as good at pretending about that as women.'

'Don't judge all women by Rosemary's standards!'

'Leave her out of it,' he said coldly.

Jealousy wouldn't be held back any longer. 'Since she's the reason for our act, I don't see how I can. Poor darling Blaize,' she said in a perfect imitation of Rosemary's lisping tones. 'I love you for the same reason I loved my poor darling Harry.'

His eyes sparked. 'What's that supposed to mean?'

'Work it out for yourself. It shouldn't take you more than ten seconds!'

She banged out of the room before he could reply and was halfway up the stairs before she remembered that she slept in the annexe. On the first landing she stopped, trying to remember how to get to the servants' quarters without going back downstairs. Slowly she walked along the corridor where the main bedrooms lay. There was a short flight of stairs at the end leading down to a sewing room. It was from here, if she remembered rightly, that one could get to the annexe. She quickened her pace, her light steps barely making a sound on the carpet. So it was that Rosemary, a vision in a diaphanous pink negligée, did not know she was being seen as she came out of her room and glided across the corridor to the door opposite. There was something so furtive in the way she moved that Miranda drew back into one of the many alcoves that the corridor possessed. As she continued to watch, Rosemary opened the door and murmured Blaize's name. Receiving no reply, she drew back and returned to her own room. Only as her door closed did Miranda step out from the alcove. She was trembling with an emotion she could not clarify, for it was compounded of many different ones: anger, jealousy and astonishment at Rosemary's effrontery. Had she gone to Blaize's room to talk to him alone or to prove she still had physical power over him? From her attire, the latter motive seemed far more likely. So much for Blaize's assertion that Rosemary had only been pretending when she had said she did not believe he was engaged to anyone else. Not only did she disbelieve it, but, in going to his bedroom, she was prepared to prove her disbelief.

Quickly Miranda raced to the sewing room and through to the annexe. Without giving herself time to think she flung off her clothes and donned a housecoat. It was a new one and she had packed it because, for a fleeting moment, she had seen herself ill, with a distraught Blaize pacing the room until she rose from her bed, beautiful in swirling aquamarine silk. How ludicrous these thoughts were now! Fastening the last button, she sped back the way she had come.

As she reached the main corridor and was a few yards from Rosemary's bedroom, she walked on the parquet edge instead of on the thick carpet that ran along the centre. The sound of her heels was audible and as she stopped by Blaize's bedroom she looked theatrically from left to right, catching a glimpse of pink silk from the corner of her eye. Rosemary had seen her! With another pantomime gesture of furtiveness, Miranda turned the handle of Blaize's bedroom door and went in. The lamp by his bed was switched on and he was lying against the pillows, reading. Hearing the door click, he looked up, his serious expression changing to one of incredulity as he saw her.

120

'Miranda!'

From the corridor behind her Miranda heard a soft step, and she made her voice louder. 'Blaize, dearest, I'm sorry to keep you waiting, but I didn't want anyone to see me. Oh, darling!' she breathed throatily, and then turned the key sharply in the lock. From the other side came silence, and only then did she move over to the bed. 'That should convince Goldilocks our engagement is real,' she concluded drily.

'You mean all that was for——' He flung out his hand and then dropped it again.

'You didn't think I meant it, did you?' she said haughtily.

His look was sardonic. 'These days one can never be sure.'

'Well, you can be sure of me, Blaize Jefferson. If I ever decide to seduce somebody it will be a *man*!'

'If you doubt that I am——' he said menacingly, and drew back the bedclothes. She jumped back so fast that he grinned. 'Don't worry,' he said wolfishly, 'I go topless, but I do wear trousers!'

Colour stained her cheeks. 'Don't try to embarrass me, Blaize. I'm here to help you, remember?'

He settled himself back in the bed and folded his arms across his chest. The movement made the muscles ripple visibly. She had no means of knowing whether he was really wearing trousers—from this angle he looked completely nude. What a wonderful body he had: the skin tanned golden and a triangular patch of black hair on his chest. There was not an ounce of superfluous flesh on him, yet he was not thin. Just ideal, she thought wearily, and knew that from now on she would always compare him with every other man she met.

'What gave you the idea of coming to my bedroom?' he asked.

'I saw Rosemary come into your room,' she said bluntly. She knew she had succeeded in surprising him. 'I was on my way to the annexe and——'

'Through the main house?' he stated disbelievingly. 'Come, come, Miranda, why not be honest and admit you were snooping?'

Her cheeks flamed again. 'It wouldn't have required any snooping to know what Goldilocks had in mind.'

'Are you telling me you came here to save me from myself?'

'Isn't that why we're engaged?' she said bluntly. 'And there's no point in my being your fiancée during the day if you're another woman's lover during the night!'

His lips twitched and he bit on the lower one as if he were trying not to laugh. 'You're as apt with a telling phrase as you are at concocting a dish,' he said dryly.

'Well, I'm stopping *your* goose from being cooked!' she retorted. 'If Rosemary had come in here in her pink nightgown you'd have been a dead duck!'

'We *are* going through the poultry tonight,' he said pleasantly. 'Have you quite finished concluding what sort of bird I would have become?'

She nodded, suddenly tired of the whole situation. 'I don't care what you do with your life. If you want to throw it away on a selfish little——'

'I'd rather we didn't discuss Rosemary's unworthiness.'

'You still defend her!' she stormed.

'Let's say I'm defending my own right to love whom I want.' He put his hands behind his head and his biceps swelled. 'However, I do appreciate your coming here like this. It's a sacrifice that smacks of the vestal virgins.' His eyes moved over her perfectly proportioned body. 'But I believe they were all as fair as you are dark,' he continued softly, 'though I'm sure the innocence in their eyes was equal to the innocence in yours.'

'I must write down your compliments, Blaize. I could sell them for Valentine cards!'

'Don't be rude,' he said abruptly. 'I meant what I said.' He dropped his hands to his sides and sat forward, his skin glistening as it caught the glow from the lamp beside him. 'Do you propose staying here the whole night?' he asked.

'Of course not,' she said promptly. 'Just long enough to—to——'

'To what?' he asked blandly.

'To let anyone watching the room think that we—er—er——'

'Have made passionate, demanding and infinitely satisfying love?'

'Oh, do shut up!' she said crossly. 'Anyway, it probably wouldn't be infinitely satisfying. I believe it rarely is the first time.'

'Don't you know?'

'You know I don't,' she said, and then stopped, realising she had walked into his trap.

Unexpectedly he gave a low chuckle and reaching out his hands, caught hold of hers and drew her down to sit on the bed.

'I'm a swine to bait you like this, but you are a pleasure to tease.' He half turned his head and looked at the small gold clock on his bedside table. 'Stick it out for another half an hour and then you can go.' He looked back at her, mocking again. 'Though if it were for real, you'd be lucky to get out before dawn!'

This time she was prepared for his teasing. 'Do you have a book I can read?' she asked.

His mouth dropped open. 'Why do you want a book?'

'To pass the time. It's boring sitting here like this.'

Disbelievingly he shook his head. 'I never thought I'd see the day when a beautiful young girl says she's bored being in my bedroom!' His eyes glinted. 'I'm sure I can occupy

123

your time far more instructively than a book.'

'But I can close the book when I want.'

'You can do the same with me,' he said. 'All you have to do is say no.'

Miranda parted her lips to say that very word when he pulled her forward and covered her mouth with his own. He was too quick for her to offer any resistance and, at his touch, she felt the tell-tale desire for him that his closeness always aroused. His chest was warm against her thin silk housecoat and she could feel the rough tangle of hairs on his breastbone as he pressed her back against the bed. She tried to resist him, but her strength was puny against his and the mattress gave way beneath her as he rolled over and half lay upon her. They could have been together on their sun-mattresses by the pool, but the lateness of the hour and the knowledge that this was the bedroom lent greater intimacy to their closeness. Blaize's lips moved gently backwards and forwards on hers, their touch as light as his fingers which nimbly undid the rhinestone buttons that glittered at the quick rise and fall of her breasts. Then his hand moved down to touch them and she gave a convulsive shudder, as though she had been kicked in the stomach. It was a sensation she had never experienced before and she tried to pull back from him, but her long skirt, which had fanned out around her as she lay down, was pinned beneath his body and held her prisoner.

Gently he went on kissing her, not forcing her, just seemingly content to rest upon her and to move his hands lightly over her shoulders and small firm breasts. And how firm they were as desire for him swelled them. With a murmur he lowered his head and rested his mouth in the shadowy curve between them. Again she shivered, and this time he reacted to it. Raising himself up, he once more took possession of her mouth, demanding her surrender. The sudden change of mood frightened her, making her realise how

124

tenuous was her control of the situation. Once one reached a certain emotional level it was difficult to draw back, and only the memory of why she was here—that this whole scene was based on a lie—gave her the impetus to push her hands hard against his chest.

'No!' she breathed, not sure if he was aware of the sound with his lips covering hers.

But he did hear the plea and slowly he drew away from her until his eyes came into focus: narrow grey-green irises with the pupils dark and enlarged. 'You see,' he whispered, 'I told you all you need do is say no.'

Lowering her lashes, she carefully slid away from him, smoothing her skirt and quickly fastening the buttons of her bodice.

'I'm not going to apologise,' he said huskily. 'If I said I was sorry for what happened, I'd be lying.'

'I'm not sorry either,' she admitted, standing. 'I think it will be in order for me to leave now, don't you?'

For an instant he was nonplussed, then he gave a soft chuckle. 'I should think so. You've been here long enough for me to have seduced you twice over!' He stood up and padded beside her to the door. Even in bare feet he towered above her, and the top of her head barely reached his chin.

'An adorable little pint pot,' he said in an unexpectedly shaky voice. 'Thanks for helping me, Miranda.'

'My mother instinct,' she retorted.

'You weren't very motherly a moment ago.'

'You weren't very fatherly.'

'I might easily have become one!'

'Blaize!' she said, and then giggled. 'Another crack like that and I'll leave you to Goldilocks.' The moment she said the word, the humour left his face. For the few moments she had been in his arms she knew he had forgotten Rosemary, but like a fool she had brought the girl to his mind. Still, it was as well for her to know how easily his mood could be changed. If she did not remember this she might read more than he meant into his kisses. She unlocked the door and opened it. The one opposite her was closed, but because the corridor was unlit she saw the sliver of light beneath it. Heartlessly she pointed to it and Blaize followed her finger and then shrugged.

'Goodnight, dearest,' Miranda said in clear tones, turning to face Rosemary's bedroom door to make sure the words were audible. 'You were wonderful!'

Hard fingers gave her a sharp nip and she squealed and turned indignantly. 'So were you, Miranda sweetheart,' Blaize replied, and remained leaning against the door jamb as she whirled smartly away down the corridor.

CHAPTER NINE

ANN, coming to Sunday lunch—for Mark had flown to Rome for a business conference—had been forewarned by her brother of his engagement to Miranda. She acted as if she had known about it the whole time, but when lunch was over she came to the kitchen for a quick word alone with her.

'You're an absolute brick to play along with Blaize,' she said.

'I didn't have much choice,' Miranda confessed.

'So Blaize told me. But even so I can't tell you how pleased I am. I would do anything to stop Rosemary getting her claws into him again.'

'I can't pretend to be engaged to him for ever. Blaize will have to fight his own battles sooner or later.'

'If only your engagement *were* real. I've a good mind to tell him I——'

'You'll tell him nothing of the sort,' Miranda interrupted. 'I've agreed to pretend for a few weeks, but I won't do it for longer.'

'Why not? Don't you like him?'

'That's beside the point.'

'On the contrary, it's the whole point,' Ann insisted. 'You can't throw him to the wolves—I mean vixen!'

'Why doesn't someone think about me for a change?' Miranda snapped. 'All this concern for Blaize! If he were half a man he'd have thrown Rosemary out yesterday instead of welcoming her into his home like the prodigal daughter!'

'I hadn't realised you were annoyed about it,' Ann said slowly. 'I took it for granted that you liked him and didn't mind helping him.'

'Of course I like him,' Miranda almost cried with frustration. 'It's because I like him that I'm so furious with him.'

Understanding dawned in Ann's eyes. 'What a chump I am! You're in love with Blaize, aren't you?'

'Don't be silly.'

'You are. That's why you agreed to help him and that's why you're furious with him. Oh, Miranda, if only Blaize would fall in love with you it would solve everything.'

'I don't want to be loved because I'm the answer to a problem,' Miranda said tartly.

'If Blaize knew how you felt it might——'

'He mustn't know,' Miranda cut in swiftly, 'and if you so much as breathe a hint of it I'll break the engagement!'

Immediately Ann swore not to say a word, but frequently during the afternoon Miranda felt Ann's eyes upon her, and realised that the sooner she left here, the better. Mrs. Holden was due back in the morning and there was no reason why she could not go to London tonight, but this of course depended on Blaize. He was talking to Rosemary and writing something down in a notebook, the dark head bent towards the golden one.

'Blaize!' she called, and watched as he straightened to look at her. 'Are we going back to London tonight or in the morning?'

'The morning. I'd like to leave soon after eight.'

'Why so early?' Rosemary questioned.

'There's no reason for *you* to leave at that time.'

'Don't be silly, darling. What would I do here without you?'

'I'm going up to London tomorrow, Rosemary,' Ann said in an expressionless voice. 'You can drive up with me.'

Irritation flitted over the doll-like face and then was gone. 'How sweet of you, Ann. That would be lovely.' She glanced at Blaize. 'I must see about finding a furnished flat till I get something permanent. I loathe staying in a hotel. It's so lonely. I had hoped to stay with you, but as you're engaged....'

'Very much engaged,' Miranda said, and looked defiantly at Blaize, knowing full well that he had been on the verge of succumbing to Rosemary's plea.

Ann stood up, explaining that it was her nanny's evening off and she had to go home to feed the baby. 'You must come over some time and meet Mark junior,' she said to Rosemary.

'I'd adore to see him,' Rosemary said. 'What's wrong with now?'

Ann looked startled at such a swift response and watched sourly as Rosemary went up to her room to collect her coat. 'Just when you think she's a cat,' she muttered to Miranda, 'she turns into a loveable little kitten.'

'Kittens have claws,' Miranda warned.

'But *you* are the scratching post,' Ann grinned, 'not me!'

Behind them, Blaize said something inaudible but bad-tempered and strode from the room, his action making it quite clear that he found their discussion of Rosemary offensive.

'My brother's an idiot,' Ann mouthed, and followed him into the hall.

Miranda remained where she was. The day had been long and tiring, the more so as her sleep the night before had been fitful. Several times she had awoken to imagine herself in Blaize's arms and each time her longing to be with him had made it difficult to fall asleep again. She strolled over to the window and looked out across the lawn. The late afternoon sun shone full into the pool, turning the water into a sheet of orange flame. There was a step behind her and she knew Blaize had come back.

'They've gone,' he said matter-of-factly. 'It's been one hell of a day!'

'You thought so too?' she said in surprise, turning to look at him.

'Naturally I dislike pretence.'

She saw he looked tired and was about to suggest he had a rest when he took his notebook from his pocket and thumbed through the pages. 'It seems to me Rosemary might be better advised to sell all her shares in Dorsen's companies. She'll either have to do that or take an active part in running them.'

'I'm sure she has the brains to do it,' Miranda replied.

'How little you know her.' Blaize returned the notebook to his pocket. 'Don't read more into her self-confidence than is there. She's an innocent when it comes to business matters.'

'But clever enough to be left her husband's money when they were supposed to be getting a divorce. Doesn't it strike you as odd?'

'Certainly not.' Blaize gave her a look of dislike. 'Harry didn't want a divorce. He was hoping Rosemary would change her mind and go back to him.'

'If she ever left.' Miranda saw the blue eyes turn frosty.

129

'If you believe her story about leaving her husband, then you'll believe anything! You might as well end our phoney engagement and marry her right away. She's obviously going to get you sooner or later.'

'I have no intention of letting anyone get me. I intend to be in control of my own happiness.'

He slumped down in a chair, looking so tired that Miranda guessed he too had had a restless night. Unwilling to have him sit here and brood upon his lost love—who was all too willing to be found again—she tried to think of a way of keeping him with her without making it look obvious.

'Help me to make supper,' she said.

His head jerked up. 'Where are the staff?'

'Gone to a charity concert in Shoreham. José and Maria wanted to stay behind, but I wouldn't let them.' She held out her hand. 'Show me how well you can break eggs.'

Blaize looked puzzled. 'Break eggs?'

'For an omelette. You can't make an omelette without breaking eggs.'

'One can apply that to most things in life,' he said ruefully as he followed her out of the room. 'Defending myself against Rosemary has meant my hurting you, although I hadn't realised it would.'

'You haven't hurt me, Blaize. I was just disappointed in your weakness.'

'But that hurt you, didn't it?' he said quietly, and, not trusting herself to speak, Miranda nodded.

Blaize proved himself remarkably adept in the kitchen and insisted on making the coffee after supper. Then they returned to the library where they read the Sunday papers. Miranda found it bitter-sweet to be so close to him yet have to hide her love. He had never looked more handsome, his body lean and strong in tight-fitting slacks and a silk jersey sweater that bore the stamp of the best Italian knitwear. All

130

his clothes were expensive, as were his accessories: wafer-thin gold watch and alligator strap, gold cutter for the cigars he smoked and a thin gold pencil which he carried about with him everywhere and had a habit of twirling idly between his hands. He was holding it as he did the crossword puzzle, a frown on his face as he searched for an elusive clue. How wonderful it would be if she could curl up in his arms instead of having to put herself as far away from him as possible.

By ten o'clock she decided it was a reasonable time to go to bed, though she was far from sleepy and knew she would lie wakeful for hours. She pretended she had her packing to do and if Blaize knew she was making an excuse to retire, he let it pass.

'Eight o'clock tomorrow,' he reminded her as she reached the door. 'I have a nine-thirty appointment at the Bank.'

'I'm never late,' she said.

'It's the rare woman who isn't.'

'I'm one of the rare ones!'

'I rather think you are,' he said slowly. 'For a pint pot you have unexpected depths.'

It was not the most romantic of compliments, but she hugged it to herself as she lay in bed, and thought of it again when she awakened next morning. True to her word she was waiting for Blaize before he himself was ready to leave, and at ten past eight they swept down the drive to the winding lane that would lead them to the motorway and London. Resolutely Miranda refused to turn for the last glimpse of the house. She doubted if she would be seeing it again and there was no point focusing it in her mind's eye. The sooner she forgot about it the better, as it would be better to forget Blaize Jefferson. But it was difficult to do this while their phoney engagement continued, and she asked him how long it would be before they could end it.

'If your bank is going to handle Rosemary's affairs she's

bound to find out our engagement is a farce.'

'I would still prefer to delay her knowing it for as long as possible. I know you think I'm weak, but stronger men than myself have made a fool of themselves over a woman. I know Rosemary's faults—no one knows them better—but it doesn't stop me loving her.'

At his words a sharp physical pain stabbed through Miranda. It was the first time Blaize had confessed his feelings so openly and it made her realise the futility of her own. 'If you know what she is,' she cried, 'how can you love her?'

'Because love isn't logical. I haven't seen her since the day she went to Africa, yet when she walked into my house it was as if I had seen her yesterday. She hadn't changed at all.'

'Neither have you. You're as stupid now as you were five years ago!'

'You've never been in love,' he said quietly. 'You don't know what it can do to you.'

'Yes, I do!' she said involuntarily, and felt him give her a quick glance.

'Do you, Miranda? Is there an unrequited love in *your* past?'

'In the present,' she said bitterly.

'I'm sorry. I hadn't realised.' They drove for a mile in silence. 'Is he married?' Blaize asked. 'Is that why he can't marry you?'

'What makes you think he wants to?'

'I took it for granted that if a man were free. . . .' He gave her another quick glance. 'You're very lovely, you know. Beautiful, in fact.'

'I'll know where to come if I want a testimonial,' she said lightly, and then added: 'Ann knows our engagement is a pretence, but what about your friends?'

'My friends?' he queried.

'If our engagement was genuine I'd surely meet them, wouldn't I? In fact if you want to convince Rosemary we aren't lying, you should give a party and introduce me to them.'

'I don't think we need be quite so precipitate,' he said carefully, 'though I agree we should put on some show.'

'Don't you want *anyone* to know the truth, apart from Ann?'

'Whom do you have in mind?'

She hesitated. 'I suppose I was thinking of Alan.'

'Ah!'

There was a wealth of meaning in the sound and she slewed round in her seat. 'Why such a portentous sound?'

'Because you've given yourself away.'

It took no leap of the imagination to know he had jumped to the conclusion that Alan was the man for whom she was secretly pining. Her immediate reaction was to deny it, but even as she opened her mouth, she stopped. Why shouldn't she let Blaize think she was in love with Alan? It would at least prevent him from guessing the truth.

'Don't worry,' Blaize went on, 'your secret is safe with me.'

'That's very kind of you,' she said carefully. 'I wouldn't want him to know.'

She saw Blaize frown and waited for his next question. When it came it illustrated his acute intelligence.

'Alan is obviously keen on you. I wouldn't have thought it would take much effort on your part to bring him up to scratch.'

'He'll scratch all right,' she retorted, 'but not legally!'

He chuckled and turned it quickly into a cough. 'Most men are scared of marriage. Perhaps your being engaged to me will put him on his mettle. There is nothing like jealousy for making a man realise what he is missing.'

'That's exactly what I thought,' she lied.

'Then I take it you won't want me to tell Alan the truth?' Blaize said.

Miranda knew she had to agree with his suggestion, though privately she decided to tell Alan the real position. 'You're quite right,' she said aloud. 'It will do him good to think our engagement is real.'

Satisfied that all foreseeable problems were solved, neither of them spoke any more, and only as they neared London did Blaize ask where he could drop her.

'The nearest Tube,' she said. 'I'm going to the flat. I don't know what Barbara has lined up for me this week.'

'Of course. I'd forgotten Miss Robinson is back at the Bank. Does that mean you'll cook for some other lucky lunch room?'

'Or go back to doing the shopping.' She made a face. 'I hate getting up so early.'

'Then don't.'

'I haven't any say in the matter. Barbara is the boss.'

'If you were a freelance, you could cook for one lunch room the whole time,' he commented. 'Why stay with your friend?'

'Because I share a flat with her and because I like her.'

He stopped at some traffic lights. 'I have half an hour to spare. Tell me where you live and I'll take you there.' She gave him the address and he headed towards it as if he knew the district well. 'I had a girl-friend who used to live close by,' he explained when she remarked on it.

'I didn't think you had any girl-friends after Rosemary.'

'Not any serious ones. I was determined to remain a bachelor.'

'You must be pleased that I'm in love with Alan.' He looked surprise and she added: 'At least you know I haven't any designs on you!'

It was a moment before he answered, and when he did

his voice was stiff. 'I never thought you had, Miranda. We're—we're attracted to each other, but that's only normal. You're beautiful and desirable and——'

'So are you!' she teased, knowing that humour was her best defence.

He laughed and stopped the car outside her block of flats. 'I'm tied up this evening, I'm afraid, but I'm free tomorrow. If you are, I suggest we have dinner together. Will eight o'clock suit you?'

'Perfectly. I'll see you then.'

Alone in the flat she changed into slacks, unpacked her case and sat down to wait for Barbara's return. Her friend was doing the marketing this week and it would be eleven before she had made all her deliveries and twelve before she was home again.

It was exactly noon when Barbara did come in, and over a light lunch she questioned Miranda about her stay in Sussex, listening goggle-eyed to the story of Rosemary's arrival and becoming incoherent when she learned of Miranda's pseudo-engagement.

'You can't ... no, it's not. ... I don't believe it!' she spluttered. 'I've heard of a woman loving a man to distraction, but never the other way round. Are you sure he isn't soft in the head?'

Forced into a defence of Blaize, Miranda was also forced to come to an appraisal of him. 'He's a romantic. He hides it in his business life, but he obviously can't do so in his private one.'

'I wouldn't describe him as a romantic,' said Barbara. 'He's just making a complete ass of himself over a worthless girl!'

'He knows Rosemary's faults, but he can't stop loving her.'

'He's mouthing words he doesn't believe. I'm sure he still thinks her parents forced her to jilt him and marry big

135

money. He won't accept she's a mercenary little gold-digger.'

'Well, that's his problem,' Miranda said shortly. 'I'm only helping him out till he decides what to do.'

'He'll marry her, of course: that's obvious. Getting engaged to you is only putting off the evil day.'

Miranda could not deny this and, to combat her sense of futility, she telephoned Alan. As a director he sat in the same room as Blaize and as he came on the line she quickly told him not to mention her name.

'He's in his private office at the moment,' Alan said softly, 'so tell me what's wrong.'

'Nothing is wrong. I'd just like to see you—without Blaize knowing.'

'Why?'

'That's what I want to see you about. Are you free to-night?'

'I can make myself free.'

'Come here for supper,' she said, unwilling to go out with him lest by some mischance Blaize saw them together.

'Cooking supper is a busman's holiday for you,' Alan protested.

'Catch the bus at eight-thirty,' she said, and hung up.

'I would never have believed Blaize would do such a thing,' Alan said much later that evening when, replete after an excellent dinner, Miranda told him of her engagement. 'It was obviously a spur-of-the-moment decision for him.'

'It might do the trick,' she said doubtfully, hoping he would agree.

'Never. If Rosemary is out to get him, he won't stand a chance.'

Since Barbara had said exactly the same, Miranda's sense of futility increased. 'Do you think I should tell Blaize to call it off?' she asked.

'Obviously I would be happier if you did. You know how I feel about you, Miranda. I was hoping you felt the same way about me.'

'We hardly know each other,' she pointed out.

'How long does it take to fall in love?'

How long had it taken her to fall in love with Blaize? She could not pinpoint the exact time, but she knew she had been intensely aware of him from their first meeting. 'I don't love you, Alan,' she said regretfully.

'Are you in love with Blaize? Is that why you agreed to his ridiculous suggestion?'

'I agreed because I thought it might help him.'

'A moment ago you said you didn't think it would.'

'I keep changing my mind,' she said quickly. 'Anyway, it's worth taking a chance if it will stop him from marrying that....'

'So you don't like Rosemary either?' he teased. 'I have yet to meet the woman who does!'

'I don't think Rosemary cares what women think of her.' Feeling she had talked enough about a girl she disliked, Miranda asked Alan to tell her what he had done in the past week. He was on the board of several companies and, being a good mimic, vividly brought to life the meetings he had attended.

'You should have been on the stage,' she said after he had given a particularly uproarious impersonation of a doddering chairman.

'That's why I went into the City!' he grinned. 'You need to be a good actor there too. Which reminds me, am I also supposed to believe in your phoney engagement?'

Miranda bit her lip. She had been waiting for this question and had already planned her answer, but now she found it more difficult to explain than she had anticipated.

'Only Ann knows it's a pretence. Blaize doesn't want anyone else to guess.'

'He's bound to tell me,' Alan said confidently. 'We don't have secrets from each other.'

'He won't tell you,' she said firmly.

'Why do you say that?'

'Because I—because I asked him not to do so. I—er—implied that I'm in love with you.'

Alan's mouth fell open and it was a moment before he recovered his equilibrium. 'You mean you want Blaize to think you love *me*?' It was half statement, half question, and he did not wait for her to answer it. 'There's only one reason why a woman would do that. You *are* in love with him, aren't you?'

'No. I only pretended about you because I thought it would make him less nervous.'

'Nervous of what?'

'That I might fall for *him*. You know how paranoic he is about being trapped into marriage. At least this way he feels safe.'

'Poor devil,' Alan said gloomily. 'When a man feels safe with a woman that's when he should start worrying!'

'Don't expect me to feel sorry for him,' she said tartly. 'Any man stupid enough to carry a torch for Rosemary deserves what he gets.'

'Well, as long as he doesn't get you, I don't mind.' Alan caught her hand and pulled on it sharply, causing her to tumble into his lap. 'I love you,' he said huskily. 'You're far too good for my best friend!'

'How loyal you are,' she quipped, and turned her head away to avoid his kiss. But he refused to be put off so easily and catching hold of her hair, made it painful for her to turn away any further. Deliberately she relaxed and let him kiss her, hoping that the feel of another man's mouth would make her realise how silly she was being over Blaize. After all, there was nothing exceptionally different about him. He was a man like any other. A little more exciting, a little better-looking perhaps, but basically no different from Alan. Yet there was a world of difference in the emotion she experienced and, with Alan's hands on her, her body longed for Blaize, making it impossible for her to simulate any response. Like a zombie she accepted Alan's embrace and, because he was not an insensitive man, he became aware of it and drew back.

'You do love Blaize,' he said flatly, 'don't bother denying it.'

'I don't know how it happened,' she said miserably.

'I'm in the same boat,' he said glumly. 'You have as much chance of success with Blaize as I have with you.'

'Oh, Alan, I hadn't seen it like that.' The knowledge that he felt as miserable about her as she did over Blaize made her long to comfort him, but because she was afraid he might misconstrue the gesture and start hoping again, she jumped to her feet and smoothed her hair. 'You won't tell him, will you?'

'Of course not.' He rose and looked into her eyes. 'What a fool he is! He has the loveliest girl under his nose and he's too blind to see her.' He buttoned his jacket and went to the door.

'We're still friends, aren't we?' she called.

Even across the room she saw him smile. 'You're as bad as Rosemary: you don't love me, but you don't want to give me up.'

'I'm sorry,' she said contritely.

'There's no need to be. As long as you aren't married to anyone else, I'll go on hoping.'

The door closed and Miranda sat down and thought of the strange triangle she and Alan and Blaize represented, with Rosemary as the hard centre around which they pivoted.

CHAPTER TEN

MIRANDA was as excited as a schoolgirl preparing for her first date as she dressed to go out with Blaize the next evening. Considering she had been involved with him in two amorous sessions she knew she was being ridiculous, but both times he had kissed her it had been because of chance, whereas tonight was planned and they would both be on their best behaviour. If only she could get him to see her with eyes that were no longer filled with a blonde image!

The bell rang and she heard Barbara go to answer it. Blaize's voice sounded in the distance and she tingled with pleasure at its deep tones. She fastened dangling ear-rings into her lobes and they swung against her cheeks, drawing attention to her high cheekbones. Tonight she wore her hair away from her face, sculpted low into the nape of her neck and combed flat on the top of her head so that one was aware of her well-shaped skull. It made her look older and sophisticated, a fact which Blaize commented on as she came in and he handed her a corsage of camellias.

'If I'd known you were going to look like this, I would have brought you tiger lilies.' He grinned at the thought. 'Definitely tiger!'

Barbara eyed them both and Blaize put his hand over Miranda's shoulder. 'Lovely, isn't she?' he said.

Miranda marvelled that he could put on such an act, and though she admired him for it she also disliked him. And men had the audacity to say women were the great pretenders! 'Where are we going?' she asked. 'I'm starving!'

'Don't you know it isn't romantic to keep talking about food? You should be surfeited with love.'

'I am, but I'm also hungry!'

Chuckling, he led her to his car. It was the Rolls tonight and chauffeur-driven. 'I thought it would give me a chance to concentrate on you,' Blaize said as he climbed into the back.

'There's no one here to see you act,' she said coldly.

'I want to stop thinking of it as an act. A good actor has to believe in the part he's playing, otherwise he won't convince his audience.'

The pleasure the first part of his sentence caused died with his conclusion of it. Trust Blaize to be logical about what he was doing! Intent on convincing Rosemary he no longer loved her, he now wanted to convince himself too. And what better way of doing so than to concentrate on another woman? Humiliation and anger vied with each other and, because of her inherent fighting spirit, anger won. With a toss of her head that set her ear-rings vibrating, she gave him such a wide smile that he half backed away and said quickly: 'We're going to the Band Box. I don't know whether you like it.'

'I like anywhere with you, darling.' She leaned close to let her perfume waft over him and saw his nostrils quiver.

'What scent are you wearing? You smell like a florist's shop.'

'Better than fried onions, isn't it?'

'I never found you smelling of onions. You've always struck me as an—as an outdoor girl.' He stared at her. 'Silly really, when you look as exotic as a Spanish dancer. It's that black hair and white skin of yours.'

'I'll bring my castanets along next time,' she said, 'but tonight you'll have to be content with clicking teeth!'

He chuckled and relaxed. 'You're a funny girl, Miranda. I always forget my problems when I'm with you.'

'That's the nicest thing you've said to me.' She slid her arm through his and felt him stiffen again. But she did not let go and after a few seconds he relaxed—but tentatively, as if still bracing himself for the unexpected.

But it was *his* next gesture that was unexpected, for he put his hand into his pocket and took out a ring box. 'For you,' he said casually, and pretended not to watch as she opened it.

A marquise-shaped diamond glittered up at her like a single sparkling star. It was the most exquisite jewel she had seen and she took it out and slipped it on her finger. It was a perfect fit and she held out her hand to him.

'It's beautiful. But why?'

'We can't have an engagement without a ring.'

'Do you want me to give you a receipt for it?' she teased.

'It's yours,' he said abruptly. 'Permanently.'

Her glance was so startled that he knew at once how his remark could be misconstrued. 'I mean you can keep it when our engagement is over.'

She had no intention of doing this and said so, a remark which he accepted with a shrug. The car stopped outside the Band Box and they went down a flight of steps to the restaurant.

'We'll go straight to our table,' said Blaize. 'I always object to being made to sit in the bar.' They followed the maître to a table at the far side of the room and Miranda was aware of many eyes following them. They made a striking couple, their colouring so similar that they could have been brother and sister. She was wearing her black dress again tonight and carried a red long-fringed shawl, which was probably another reason why Blaize had likened her to a Spanish dancer.

Over the meal they talked of inconsequential things and only when they reached the coffee stage did he relax sufficiently to tell her something about his day. Miranda knew little of finance, but she enjoyed the cut and thrust of brain against brain, and Blaize explained the situation he was

142

dealing with so dramatically that it was like listening to a thriller.

'Most business is a thrill,' he said. 'That's why I chose the City in preference to a profession.'

'My father is the exact opposite,' Miranda ruminated. 'He likes everything to be cut and dried.'

'Has he always worked for Basic Oil?'

'It's the only job he's had. We're a loyal lot, the Joneses.'

'I should imagine you are.' He smiled at her. 'I like your hair that way, Miranda, but you need a red rose behind your ear.'

'Or clenched between my teeth!'

'It's only held that way when you dance the flamenco. It's a pity I didn't think to take you somewhere where there's music. I've never danced with you.'

'You'll have lots of opportunity, darling.' She knew she had startled him again, but he had quick control this time and leaning forward, drew her hands to his lips. It was a lover-like gesture and was noticed by two people coming towards them.

'Blaize,' said the man, and Blaize turned his head, dropping Miranda's hands slowly as he rose to greet him and the woman by his side. The couple glanced at Miranda, and intercepting their look, Blaize smiled. 'I don't believe you've met my fiancée, Miranda Jones?'

'I didn't even know you were engaged,' said the man.

'We kept it a secret until this weekend.'

'You dark horse!' The man clapped Blaize on the back. 'I haven't seen it in *The Times*. When are you getting married?'

'We haven't set the date yet.'

'It won't be long,' Miranda cooed.

'How wise you are,' the woman said.

'It seems to me Blaize is the wise one.' The man eyed Miranda with admiration. 'Where did you find her?'

'On top of a Christmas tree,' Miranda said before Blaize could answer. 'I'm his good fairy!'

When the couple went to their own table Blaize faced Miranda with an odd look. 'I hadn't realised how good you are at making snide remarks.'

'No one else knows I'm doing it,' she said calmly, 'only you.'

'You enjoy making fun of me, don't you?'

She pretended to concentrate on choosing a *petit four*. 'It's good for you. You take yourself too seriously.'

'I don't get much chance while you're around—which reminds me, Ann is joining Mark in town this week. She suggested we went with them to the theatre one evening.'

'I'd like that,' said Miranda. 'At least you'd be able to be natural with me for one evening.'

'I am natural with you now. I don't have to pretend I like you—I do like you.'

'I like bread and butter,' she said.

'What else do you want me to say?' he asked irritably, 'that I love you?'

'I don't expect you to lie in your private life, Blaize, I'm sure you do enough of that in your business one!'

He caught his breath. 'You really are the most provocative girl I know!'

'Do you want me to simper at you instead?' Her voice mimicked Rosemary's. 'My poor darling Blaize!'

Sparks flashed in his grey-green eyes and he bit into his own biscuit as if he would have much preferred to have bitten her. 'Don't provoke me when we're alone,' he said softly, 'or you might regret it.'

'I might take a chance and do just that,' she whispered equally softly. 'I'm a born masochist!'

His mouth curved. He attempted to straighten it, but humour won the day and he smiled openly. 'Come on, pint pot. I will take you dancing after all.'

For the rest of the week Blaize acted the perfect lover in public, though when they were alone in the car or when he came to the flat, he was his usual friendly and occasionally tetchy self.

Miranda continued to tease him, sometimes almost tormenting him, until she really did feel he had to restrain himself from slapping her. But only by teasing him could she stop herself from waxing sentimental over him, for the more she got to know him the more deeply she fell in love with him. Listening to him talk confirmed her opinion that he was an idealist, and not only in his personal life but in his business one too. Ruthless with enemies, he was a pushover with his friends and displayed a loyalty to them which she wondered if they returned. He even continued to visit the ex-chairman of the Lothian Bank who, after a severe stroke eighteen months ago, had sold his total interest in Blaize and retired to live in the country.

'He still likes to know what's going on in the City,' Blaize told her, 'and I enjoy telling him. He finds it difficult to talk since his stroke, but we've worked out a pretty good system of communication.'

'It must be awful to want to say things and not be able to speak,' commented Miranda.

'You would find it devastating,' he chuckled. 'I've never known a girl talk as much as you.'

'I must learn to hold my tongue.'

'Please don't. Your chatter amuses me.'

'Your very own Court jester. You must buy me a cap and bells.'

'I've bought you this instead.' He casually put a package on the table. They were dining in a restaurant in Soho, their table secluded from the others by a wall of greenery.

Miranda undid the wrapping and took out a narrow white gold bracelet watch. It was the daintiest thing she had seen, and because she had not expected it she was horrified to find tears filling her eyes.

'Here,' Blaize said brusquely. 'Let me put it on for you.' Catching her wrist, he did so, his fingers firm.

The bracelet fitted perfectly. 'You have a very good eye,' she mumbled. 'Even the ring didn't need any alteration.'

'I'm excellent at sizing up people!' he quipped. 'I doubt if I would be more than a centimetre out if I were to buy your lingerie.'

She blushed and was annoyed with herself. 'You shouldn't have bought me this. You embarrass me.'

'I have more money than I know what to do with,' he replied. 'I saw the watch in a window and it reminded me of you.'

Miranda stared into the little gold face but failed to see any resemblance.

'It's tiny but perfect,' he added.

His compliment was almost her undoing and she fumbled in her bag for her handkerchief. She had always presented such a picture of pert control that she was reluctant to destroy the image, but for the life of her she could not think of anything funny to say. All she wanted to do was to hug the watch and howl like a child.

'I'm going to Sussex for the weekend,' Blaize was speaking again. 'You'll come with me, of course?'

'Of course,' she said, not having thought about it until this moment. 'But is it strictly necessary?'

'Rosemary is coming for lunch on Saturday,' he replied, and his eyebrows met above his nose in a scowl. 'You were right about her, Miranda. She doesn't believe our engagement is real.'

'How do you know?'

'I had lunch with her yesterday.'

A wave of anger swamped over Miranda. To think Blaize had been with Rosemary yesterday and she herself had gone out with him last night and not even guessed! She was so intensely aware of everything about him that she had been convinced she would automatically know when he had been with another woman.

'Why did you see her?' she asked.

One eyebrow lifted at the question, but he apparently thought it a fair one, for he answered it. 'As you know, we're going to handle her affairs.'

'Ah yes. And she's either going to sell out or become a business tycoon.'

'She has decided to sell, but is leaving me to do it at the most propitious time. It will take quite a while. She has large holdings and they have to be disposed of carefully.'

'Skip the business part,' Miranda said impatiently. 'What did she say about *us*?'

With an oddly nervous gesture Blaize ran his tongue over his lips. 'It was what she implied rather than what she said.'

Miranda knew he was lying. Nothing she had so far seen in Rosemary's behaviour towards him indicated subtlety. 'I suppose she told you I'd thrown myself at you.' Miranda made the remark at random, but from Blaize's startled movement she knew it had hit home. 'I suppose she thinks I seduced you and then bludgeoned you over the head with your own chivalry?'

'Something like that,' he conceded.

'If she's staying the night on Saturday,' Miranda continued, 'perhaps we'll give her a repeat performance of last week.'

'She won't be staying the night, nor would I advise you to repeat the performance.'

'Why not? I didn't mind.'

'Don't be so trusting,' he said abruptly. 'One day you'll invite yourself into one bedroom too many.'

The idea was so ludicrous that she giggled.

'It's true,' he continued, looking angry. 'One day you'll land yourself in a tricky situation.'

'I'm not a bad judge of men,' she assured him.

'Alan is coming down too,' Blaize said abruptly, his tone showing her quite clearly that he still believed her to be in love with his friend.

'What made you ask him?'

'I thought it might help to make him jealous.'

'What a good idea! I never thought of that.'

'You need someone to take care of you.' He signalled for the bill. 'And I've designated myself as your guardian.'

Returning to the house in Sussex which she had never expected to see again, Miranda went straight to the kitchen to say hello to Mrs. Holden and the rest of the staff. They knew of her engagement and though there was a momentary embarrassment, her naturalness with them soon dissolved it.

Alan arrived in time for cocktails and Blaize went out of his way to be attentive to Miranda. Alan watched the performance with a lowering expression, but brightened when Miranda managed to whisper to him that Blaize was putting on an act to make him jealous.

'It looked pretty convincing to me,' Alan muttered. 'Make sure he doesn't get carried away with it.'

Miranda wished he would be, but diplomatically didn't say so, though she gave Blaize every encouragement when he lightly kissed her goodnight in the hall.

'I think I did very well,' he said. 'Alan has been glowering at me all evening.'

'You were wonderful,' she assured him. 'I think I'd better lock my bedroom door.'

'I beg your pardon?'

'Just in case you try and do for me what I tried to do for you last week!' she reminded him, and saw him relax as he realised she was teasing. She went towards the stairs and halfway up, glanced back, seeing he had not returned to the library for a nightcap but was watching her with an odd look on his face.

Miranda awoke early the next morning, but remained lazily in bed until voices in the garden below teased her into coming to the window. Blaize and Alan stood side by side, both in shorts, both carrying tennis rackets.

'I'll take on you and Alan,' Blaize challenged.

'I'm too lazy for tennis,' she called. 'I'll meet you by the pool afterwards.'

They went away and she put on a bikini and towelling wrap, had a glass of milk in lieu of breakfast and went to sit by the pool.

It was another glorious day, the sky blue as the Madonna's robe, the sun yellow as a new gold sovereign. Miranda relaxed back on a mattress and closed her eyes, only tensing as a foot came down and rested on her stomach.

'Blaize Jefferson!' she protested indignantly.

'How did you know it was me? You have your eyes closed.'

'I can recognise your sole!'

He laughed and bending down, scooped her up into his arms. It required great strength for him to do this, but it did not even make his breath go faster and he remained holding her, their bodies touching, hers creamy gold, his considerably darker. Slowly he set her down on her feet and stepped back, as if regretting the sudden intimacy between them. Without a word he went over to the diving board and climbed to the top. He stood poised there like a statue and then did a perfect dive into the water, coming up for air almost halfway across the pool.

More gingerly Miranda eased herself into the water and swam over to join him. Within a moment Alan was there, too, and they swam several lengths before climbing out to dry in the sun.

'This is the life for me,' she said blissfully.

'Why not stay here till the weather breaks?' Blaize suggested. 'If you do, I'll come down in the evenings.'

His suggestion surprised her, the more so since she knew it had been spontaneously made. It showed her how quickly he had accepted their relationship, acting almost as if it were a real one. 'I can't do that,' she said regretfully. 'I'll be poisoning the directors of an insurance company for the next month.'

'It's nonsense for you to go on working,' Blaize said. 'You must set a date for the wedding.'

Surprised, Miranda sat up straight. Blaize was still lying flat, his eyes closed, but Alan was sitting up and he winked at her over his friend's inert form. Miranda nodded silently to Alan, but when she spoke her tones were dulcet.

'I wish we could cut out all the fuss, darling. Why don't you get a special licence?'

This remark brought Blaize up so abruptly that his head almost hit hers. 'I might do that,' he said menacingly and, swinging her to her feet with him, threw her into the pool.

'What was that for?' she spluttered as he jumped in beside her.

'I thought you needed cooling down!'

She caught hold of the skin on his arm and nipped it viciously. He gave a yell of pain and ducked her, then brought her back to the surface, treading water and holding her clasped tightly against his chest. Her arms gripped him round the waist and her long dark hair wound itself around him.

'Little witch,' he muttered, then his lips, cold and wet, pressed hard on hers, remaining there until, forgetting to dog-paddle, they both sank below the water. Separately they rose again and Miranda turned over on her back and floated away, deliberately keeping her eyes closed until she was able to get some control of herself.

They were lying beside the pool again when Rosemary

arrived. To Miranda's annoyance she looked stunningly beautiful in a vividly patterned shirt and emerald green pants that matched the green straw hat that covered her blonde head. Watching Blaize from the corner of her eye Miranda saw a muscle twitch in his cheek, though his voice was cool as he greeted his guest and made sure she was comfortably settled.

'I bet you must be tired of sunshine,' Alan remarked.

'In Durban I hardly ever sat out in it,' Rosemary replied. 'When you know you're going to have sun for months on end, you get blasé about it.'

Miranda would have liked to ask her if having Blaize's devotion for so long had made her blasé about that too, for she could think of no other reason why Rosemary had jilted him. Could she really have preferred marriage to a middle-aged man to life with this virile, handsome one? Obviously she had, and obviously she now wanted to have the best of two worlds: her late husband's money and Blaize's love. Abruptly Miranda rose.

'Where are you going?' Blaize asked.

'To change into something dry.'

'I'll come with you.' Clasping her affectionately round the waist, he walked with her across the lawn. His hand dropped away from her as soon as they were out of sight—a fact which she noticed with a pang—and he was silent as they went into the house.

'Don't be long,' he said. 'I'll wait here for you.'

When she came down a little later, cool as a mint julep in aquamarine cotton, it was to find that he had changed too. His hair still gleamed wet and lay across his scalp as shiny as a raven's wing, while his eyes looked much darker, a tendency she had noticed before when he was tense. They strolled back to the pool and Miranda was aware of Rosemary's eyes on her, hard and sharp.

'You were a long time,' she said.

'Blame Blaize,' Miranda said in a falsely husky tone, and poured herself a fruit juice from the tray of drinks which José had brought out for them. Her engagement ring sparkled in the sunlight and Rosemary's eyes went to it like a snake to a rabbit.

'Lovely, isn't it?' Miranda cooed, and held out her finger.

Rosemary drew away from it haughtily. 'If you like diamonds.'

'I would have thought you did,' Miranda said equably.

'Not for an engagement ring. It's so banal.' Dimples flashed in Blaize's direction. 'I still have the ring you bought me, though perhaps it's naughty of me to say so.'

'Naughty but expected,' Miranda put in. 'The one thing about you, Rosemary, is that you haven't yet succeeded in surprising me.'

Blaize jumped up so abruptly that he jerked against Miranda and sent her glass flying. It crashed to the floor and a large piece jagged into her calf. Blood started to flow.

'Oh, God!' Blaize jerked out, and catching her up in his arms again, raced her towards the house.

'For heaven's sake,' she protested, 'I'm not bleeding to death!'

'Keep still,' he ordered. 'You might have a splinter in your vein.'

Instantly she went motionless, imagining a chunk of glass travelling like a needle towards her heart. He strode across the sitting room and settled her gently into a chair, enjoined her not to move and went off in search of his first-aid kit.

Miranda remained where she was, her leg stretched out motionless. Gingerly she peeped down at it. Blood oozed down her ankle, coming from a jagged cut just above the bone. What an unnecessary fuss Blaize was making! Winding her handkerchief around her leg, she went across to the hall cloakroom and dabbed the wound clean. Despite his pessimism there were no splinters in it; all she had to do now was to stop herself bleeding like a pig. The door behind her opened and Blaize stood there, irate.

'I thought I told you not to move.' Without waiting for her to reply he pushed her none too gently into a white wicker chair. He was holding the first-aid box and he took out some iodine.

'That will hurt,' Miranda protested.

'No, it won't, it's the non-stingable kind.'

She tensed, not believing him, but found he had not lied, for there was no sting as he applied the liquid, then placed some lint on her leg and held it there tightly.

'Sit still for a couple of minutes and the bleeding will stop,' he assured her.

She had no option but to obey, and was conscious of his fingers on her ankle and the ungracious picture she must make with one leg stuck up in the air like a chicken on a plate.

'You brought the whole thing on yourself,' he said unkindly. 'You shouldn't have baited Rosemary the way you did.'

'She's too thick to notice.'

'Last week,' he said thinly, 'you accused her of extreme cleverness.'

'She's clever all right,' Miranda said airily, 'but in a cunning, self-preserving way. But she's also as thick-skinned as a rhinoceros.'

'And you're as short-sighted,' he ground out, 'if you think that showing me Rosemary's faults will stop me loving her.'

'You'll never stop loving her,' Miranda cried. 'To do that, you would have to admit what a fool you'd been in the first place!' She pulled her ankle free and stood up. 'We'd better go back—otherwise Rosemary will think we're making love again!'

'Be careful what you say to her this time,' he warned.

'I'm only being your loving fiancée,' she reminded him. 'If you don't like the way I show my affection, you put on the act instead.'

His jaw clenched, but he took the hint and, as they approached Rosemary and Alan, he slowed his step and put his arm around Miranda's waist. 'I'll break your ribs if you don't behave,' he said, looking at her as tenderly as though he was whispering endearments, and she smiled up at him provocatively, yet was careful not to meet his eyes.

Alan's presence saved the lunch from being a fiasco, for Rosemary ignored Miranda and concentrated so obviously on Blaize that even he was embarrassed by it. But Miranda was glad, for it justified the accusations she had levelled at the girl.

When luncheon was over and they returned to the pool, Blaize left Alan to entertain Rosemary, while he himself tried to make conversation with Miranda. But Miranda wanted his genuine attention, not his pity, and she glared over to where the chocolate box beauty was trying to woo Alan.

'Don't be jealous,' Blaize whispered, misreading her action. 'Rosemary isn't his type.'

'I'm not in the least worried,' she snapped, but saw that Blaize did not believe her, for he sauntered over to Rosemary and suggested a stroll, leaving Alan free to join Miranda.

'How's it going?' he asked.

'You can see for yourself. Blaize was furious with me for teasing her.'

'And then he was furious with *her* for ignoring *you*.'

'He just doesn't like bad manners,' Miranda said matter-of-factly.

'I think it was more than that. He doesn't want you to be

hurt. You should have seen his face when that piece of glass went into your leg. He looked shattered.'

'Because he blamed himself. Don't expect me to believe he has any feelings for me.'

'What about your feelings for him? Are they still the same?'

'I don't change my mind so quickly.'

'Neither do I. Remember that, Miranda.'

Rosemary left after tea, driven away in a gleaming Cadillac sent for her by the American couple with whom she was staying some ten miles away.

'I knew them in Africa,' she had explained. 'He was a business associate of Harry's.' Her glance had slid to Blaize. 'I would like you to meet him. He's anxious to invest in this country. I'll arrange a little dinner party one evening next week. It's so much better to do these introductions socially.'

Blaize had nodded and, almost as if he could not help himself, had met Miranda's eyes. She had kept her face expressionless but lowered one lid deliberately, showing him that though he might not, she at least saw through Rosemary's ploy.

With Rosemary gone, the tension left the atmosphere and once again Blaize and Alan became teasing towards her, cheating outrageously when they played three-handed gin rummy, which they did until ten o'clock when they all retired for an early night.

The sun was debilitating and Miranda slept like a log, awakening to another day of bright sunshine and happy in the knowledge that this day at least would not be spoilt by Rosemary's presence. But though she did not appear she did succeed in marring the day, for at noon she telephoned to say her American friends would be coming to London on Wednesday and would Blaize dine with her then.

'Am I invited too?' Miranda asked him.

'It's a business dinner,' he said quietly, Alan's presence

155

making it impossible for him to be curt.

Alan, aware of this but pretending not to be, delighted Miranda by suggesting he took her out that night instead. 'You don't mind, do you, Blaize?' he asked.

Blaize gave Miranda a surreptitious look and then nodded vigorously. 'By all means, old chap.'

'There's supposed to be a good play at Chichester,' Alan said to Miranda. 'How do you feel about driving down?'

'You'll be doing the driving, not me.'

'It's settled, then—providing I can get the tickets—but we'll have to leave early because of the traffic.'

'I'm always free from four o'clock onwards,' said Miranda.

'Good. We'll leave at five, then.'

Later that evening Blaize had a moment alone with her. 'It looks as if it's working for you,' he said. 'Seeing you with me has made Alan wake up.'

'Yes,' she said tonelessly, and wished that seeing her with Alan would have the same effect on Blaize. But he was blinded by china blue eyes and corn gold hair and totally oblivious to the charms of a dusky Spanish beauty.

CHAPTER ELEVEN

ALAN returned to London on Sunday evening, but Blaize decided not to leave until the next morning, promising to make sure Miranda arrived in town before ten o'clock.

'It's my first day at the new lunch room and I'm a bit nervous,' she confessed as they finally set off.

'I don't believe you're ever nervous about cooking—or about anything else, for that matter.'

In one way it was gratifying to think how little he knew her, but in another way it was disheartening, and she was not sure whether to explain that not only was she nervous of cooking, but of many other things too.

'You must have been the most popular girl in your school,' he went on.

'I was the one most often in trouble,' she confessed.

'For being tactless.'

'I've been remarkably tactful lately,' she reproached him.

'Only because I've been watching you like a hawk!'

She looked at him indignantly and saw he was grinning. They had quickly returned to their normal easy friendship and Miranda marvelled at the fact that a couple of weeks ago she had not even known he existed. Yet now her whole world was bounded by him. The knowledge that in a few weeks he might already have gone from her life was enough to quench her happy mood and she lapsed into silence and stared miserably through the window. Several miles went by, and she was surprised to come out of her reverie and see they had stopped in a lay-by. Without speaking Blaize leaned over into the back of the car and lifted out a small hamper. In it was a thermos of coffee and some delicious fruit cake.

'At half-past nine in the morning?' she said in disbelief.

'Mrs. Holden told me you had no breakfast, and knowing you I'm sure you won't have time for lunch today either. Hence this little snack.' He poured out a cup of coffee and handed it to her, together with the cake. 'Put that inside you. If you get any thinner I'll be able to put you in my pocket.'

'I wish I were tall,' she said, munching.

'You're just the right size.'

She longed to ask him for whom, but thought it would be unwise.

'Will you be too tired to go out tonight?' he asked abruptly.

'I don't see why.'

'I just thought that as you're rather nervous about today's luncheon. . . .'

'I'll have recovered by this evening. Come round to the flat and you can teach me how to play backgammon.'

'You come over to mine,' he suggested. 'If I come to you, you'll end by cooking again.'

She had not been to his home yet, but knew he lived in Chelsea. 'Don't bother collecting me,' she said, 'and don't bother with dinner either.'

'I wasn't intending to stand over a hot stove myself,' he teased. 'I have an excellent housekeeper. Another Spanish couple, actually.'

'You're so well catered for I can see why you've never bothered to marry.'

The moment she had spoken she could have bitten off her tongue and she waited for him to freeze on her, but he continued to lounge back easily in his seat, sipping his coffee as if they had all the time in the world. His calm was deceptive, for he kept his eye on his watch and soon took the cup from her hand, closed the hamper and set the car in motion. He deposited her outside the majestic though gloomy headquarters of the Falcon Insurance Company with a quarter of an hour to spare, reminded her not to be late that evening and drove away.

The moment she entered the kitchen, Miranda forced Blaize out of her mind. There was work to be done and she must do it.

She did not allow him to take over her thoughts again until she paid off the taxi later that evening and went up in the small lift that only served the top floor penthouse. How typical of Blaize to have the most luxurious apartment in the building. By no dint of imagination could she imagine him making do with second best. Yet she knew from Alan that he had not always been wealthy; rich by most people's standards, maybe, but not rich enough five years ago to have prevented Rosemary from jilting him. She stabbed the doorbell as if it were a china blue eye and forced a smile to her lips as Blaize greeted her warmly. He was casual in slacks and a grey silk shirt. His hair looked ruffled and she suspected he might have been having a rest. Her suspicion was correct, for as she went into the living room she saw the cushions in disarray on the settee.

'What a beautiful room!' She admired the ivory silk-covered walls and the off-white carpet. The furnishings were colourless too, but the cushions were bright, as were the modern paintings on the walls, a Hockney above the fireplace and a Mark Rothko to her left, with others which she did not recognise.

Blaize motioned her to a chair and brought her a long cool drink. 'A Jefferson Special,' he said as she eyed it suspiciously.

She sipped it and found it delicious. 'Lovely!'

'All my women like it!'

She longed to ask if this included Rosemary, but by now she had too tight a hold over her tongue.

'No,' he said, coming to sit opposite her with a Scotch and soda in his hand, 'Rosemary didn't.'

'How did you——?'

'Your eyes can sometimes be as tactless as your tongue!'

She sniffed miffily. 'I suppose she preferred cream.'

He laughed. 'You're the one who should be served the cream! A saucerful if you go on like this. Now let's change the subject.'

'Is there any point?' she asked. 'She's always hovering in the background.'

'Rosemary isn't hovering in my background tonight,' he said firmly. 'I intend to concentrate on *you*.'

He did exactly that, giving her a second drink before leading her into the dining room. Here the colours were sombre; dark brown silk walls, black carpet and scarlet and gold lacquered Chinese furniture.

It was easy for Miranda to imagine that their engagement was a real one and that the flawless diamond she wore on her finger symptomised Blaize's love for her. It was painful to visualise him with another woman, yet she knew that inevitably there would be only one in his life and that this would be Rosemary.

Miranda's hands trembled and she set her fork down on the plate, afraid that Blaize would notice. What would her reaction be if he asked her to continue their engagement? If he suggested marriage? But no, that was a foolish thought, not even Blaize would commit himself permanently to one woman in order to escape from another.

'Why the sigh?' he asked.

'It was a purely unconscious one.'

'I'm sure your thoughts weren't unconscious, Miranda. You looked extremely pensive. Can I offer you a penny for them?'

'You'll have to do better than that in these days of inflation!' She hesitated. 'But I'll tell you anyway. I was wondering how you're going to ward Rosemary off when we break our engagement.'

He was silent for so long that she had decided that he was not going to reply, when he did so. 'Why look so far into the future, Miranda? Let's just take things as they come.'

'You can't be engaged to me for ever.'

He looked quizzical. 'Are you proposing to me?'

'Of course not,' she said promptly. 'I was thinking of Alan.'

Blaize's lower lip jutted forward. 'He didn't take his eyes off you the whole weekend.'

'You're exaggerating.'

'No, I'm not. He watched you like a cat watching a canary.'

160

'Because I'm in *your* cage! He might not do the same if I were flying free.'

'Yes, he would,' Blaize said slowly, and then gave a slight smile. 'But that's what you want, isn't it?'

She nodded and resumed eating, marvelling as she frequently did these days, that Blaize could be so blind.

Dinner over, they went to sit on the terrace. It was a miniature garden with a small tinkling fountain and numerous urns filled with trailing plants.

'In the winter when I sit in the dining room I can look out here and imagine I'm in the country. It stops me missing the house so much.'

'Don't you go down in the winter?'

'Only at weekends.'

'It's a big house for one person,' she commented.

'I have many friends and when I get especially lonely I invite someone special to keep me company.'

'It's fine to be a Casanova while you're young, but how will you manage when you're over forty?'

'As well as I do now!' he smiled. 'I'll start worrying when I'm over fifty. Which reminds me, I haven't got *your* number in my little black book!'

'Don't waste your time putting it there,' she said tartly. 'I have no intention of joining the queue.'

'As my fiancée you're at the top of it.'

'Only temporarily. You're running away from the inevitable, poor darling Blaize.'

'Stop that!' he said sharply, and leaning across the gap that divided them, gave her a sharp jerk. He didn't realise his strength nor that she was so petite, for the movement catapulted her on to his lap. Before she could jump off, his arms came round her.

'I can span your waist with my hands,' he said in surprise, and suited his action to his words. 'You're so vociferous and self-opinionated I always forget you're just a little shrimp.'

'I've got a lobster's claws,' she smiled.

'And a scorpion's sting!' His grasp tightened. 'Show me how nice you can be—instead of how nasty.' Not giving her a chance to comply, he cupped her head in his hands and brought it towards his. He did not kiss her as she expected but subjected her to a searching stare. 'You have the most unusual eyes,' he murmured, 'not just the colour but the shape. I hadn't noticed how they tilt up at the corners—a bit like a Siamese. You have the same pointed face too, with those haughty cheekbones and wilful mouth.'

'You sound as if you're taking an inventory of me.' She made an effort to hide the emotion his words aroused in her. ' "Item, two lips indifferent red," ' she quoted, ' "item, two grey eyes with lids to them." '

'*Twelfth Night*,' he said triumphantly, 'the lovely Olivia.'

'I'm glad you know your Shakespeare.'

'I know a lot more besides, my lovely Miranda. Let me show you.' Slowly his lips came towards her.

She had ample time to move, but she remained motionless and as his mouth rested upon her own, she gave an imperceptible sigh and relaxed against him. His tallness and breadth of shoulder made her feel small and she nestled close. Blaize appeared to regard it as the movement of a child and for an instant he lifted his head and gave her a tender smile before kissing her again. There was no passion in it, just warmth and comfort and a mutual ease. 'It's hard to think of you as a firecracker now,' he said huskily. 'You're like a cuddly toy.'

'Not such a toy,' she whispered.

'Maybe not.' He rubbed the tip of his tongue gently over her lips. His hold tightened and what had begun as a tentative kiss became an exploratory one. Regretting her initial response, Miranda set her lips together, but with determined pressure he parted them. She trembled and gave way to the emotion that flooded through her body. This was Blaize who was holding her, the man she loved, the man with whom she would be happy to share the rest of her life. The knowledge overwhelmed her and the sadness of realising it would never come to pass lent greater poignancy to the pleasure of the moment. With total abandon she reponded to his touch, making no protest when his hands moved over her body like a musician on his instrument; and how subtly he played; knowing how to get the best response, when to be gentle, when to be strong, proving himself a veritable master at the game of love. For that was all it was to him, she knew—a game.

Without being aware of it she was lying full length on the settee and Blaize was beside her, holding her as if he would never let her go. She was trapped beneath the weight of his body, but she knew no sense of fear, not even when he pulled down the bodice of her dress and pressed his mouth to her small, uptilted breasts. It was only as his hand pushed her skirt aside and moved along the curve of her hip that she gave a shiver and went to push him away. Instantly his hand drew back and came up to caress the dark hair that lay like a silky cap against her scalp.

'You're beautiful, Miranda. Beautiful and seductive.' He placed gentle little kisses across her forehead and down her temple to her ear, then let his tongue play with the lobe. 'I want you,' he said quietly.

'So I've gathered.'

'I don't suppose you would care to say yes?'

She rubbed her cheek against his and spoke directly on his lips. 'I would love to say yes, but I can't ... I never have.'

'I know.' His grip tightened. 'I'll be jealous of the man who makes you change your mind. He'll have to be a fool not to know how lucky he is.'

She longed to tell him that he was the fool, and knew how astonished he would be if she did. But then his astonishment would give way to pity and perhaps to the fear that she had agreed to this false engagement in the hope of trapping him into marriage. If only she had the courage to do such a thing! Married to her, Blaize would be far less unhappy than he was certain to be with Rosemary, who would marry him only to use him. The thought of Rosemary was like frost on a flower and Miranda curled up within herself, withering the way petals do when they die. Blaize sensed her withdrawal, but not knowing the reason, assumed it to be fear.

'Don't be scared, Miranda. I've never yet taken a girl by force.'

The words reminded her that though he still yearned for Rosemary he had not lived like a monk. Yet she was far less jealous of the other women in his life than of the one scheming blonde whom she knew. Impotent anger brought her into a sitting position.

'It's late, I must go.'

'I'll drive you back.'

'Don't bother. Just call me a cab.'

He did not reply and instead stood up, stretched lazily and led her across to the lift. They rode down in silence, but in the car she recovered her equilibrium and by the time they reached her flat they were chatting as easily as they had been earlier in the evening.

'I have a business dinner tomorrow,' said Blaize as he walked with her to the entrance.

'You have one on Wednesday too.'

He flashed her a look. 'So I have.'

'Monkey business,' she added.

'Hank Schneider is an important man,' Blaize said stiffly. 'It was very thoughtful of Rosemary to arrange the meeting.'

'She's full of thoughtfulness. You'd better make sure she doesn't pack Mr. Schneider off early. You might not have as much control over your emotions as I do over mine.'

'You despise me for being weak, don't you?' he said abruptly.

'I despise you for being blind,' she corrected and before he could think of a suitable answer, pushed open the glass door and let it swing behind her.

Lying in bed, she could not help wondering what would have happened if she had acceded to Blaize's request that evening. Yet to have allowed their love to come to total fruition would have created far more problems than it would have solved. It might even have told him that she loved him. The very thought made her shiver. But had Rosemary guessed it? On Saturday those china blue eyes had watched her appraisingly, and Miranda knew it would take more than a diamond ring to convince the girl that Blaize was no longer hers for the asking.

Miranda did not hear from Blaize on Tuesday or Wednesday, though Alan rang to confirm that he would be picking her up at five and, true to his word, was waiting for her when she came down at the appointed time.

They did not speak much until they had weaved their way through the worst part of the rush hour traffic, but once on the open road they both relaxed and spoke of anything and everything except Rosemary and Blaize.

Miranda knew Alan was waiting for her to broach the subject first, but she was curious to see if she could spend an evening with another man without thinking of the one she loved. It was impossible, of course; even sitting beside Alan reminded her of Blaize, and she wished it were possible to transport herself across space and time and be back in his penthouse and held close in his arms.

'I hope the play is worth the journey,' Alan said.

'It might have been easier if we'd gone by train.'

'I don't mind driving. It relaxes me.' He gave her an oblique glance. 'You don't look very relaxed, though. Sorry you agreed to come with me?'

'Don't be silly. I'm not going to sit at home pining for Blaize.' Miranda bit her lip, annoyed that after all she had been the first one to mention his name.

'I won't waste my breath asking if you still love him.'

'Good.' She clenched her hands. 'Let's talk about something else. I haven't come out with you to spend the evening worrying whether Blaize is making an ass of himself.'

Accepting the dictum, Alan regaled her with various business stories, some true, some exaggerated, but all amusing. By the time they reached Chichester, Miranda was totally relaxed. She had even forgotten that Blaize was by now in Rosemary's home, sitting at her table and smiling into her eyes.

'Come back to me, Miranda!' Alan called.

With a start of confusion she did so, annoyed that her thoughts could so easily play her traitor. It had taken them longer to reach the theatre than they had anticipated and they only had time for a drink before the curtain went up. But the interval was a long one and they were able to dine lightly though well in the theatre restaurant. Then they returned to see the end of the play and by ten-thirty they were once more heading towards London.

They made good time on the almost deserted road and the accident, when it came, came with the suddenness of lightning. One moment they were speeding along the highway with no vehicle in front or behind them, and the next a car was hurtling towards them, its headlights blazing. Alan swung the wheel sharply, at the same time slamming his foot on the brake. The car shuddered and reared up in the air, then careered halfway across the road to crash into a hedge, while the other car slewed round in a circle and thudded into a concrete bollard.

'Are you all right, Miranda?' Alan's voice was a thin thread of sound.

'Yes,' she said shakily, knowing that if she had not been wearing her seat belt the sudden braking would have sent her hurtling through the windscreen.

'The man must be a maniac,' Alan muttered, and wrenching open the door, stumbled across the road to see what had happened.

Quickly Miranda followed, her stomach muscles tightning as she neared the wreckage of the other car and saw its driver lying sprawled on the road.

'Is he dead?' she asked shakily.

'No,' Alan reassured her, 'but we'd better get him to a hospital. He's bleeding badly.' He straightened. 'And drunk, of course. He reeks of whisky.'

Miranda looked to see if there was a callbox nearby and Alan pointed behind him. 'We passed one about fifty yards back. I don't know what made me notice it. You wait here while I telephone for help.' He hurried off and Miranda looked at the man at her feet. He was still unconscious and breathing heavily. She bent to feel his pulse and was still kneeling beside him when Alan returned.

'I got the local police,' he said. 'They'll be along with an ambulance.'

Within a few moments a police car, its blue light flashing, came to a stop beside them, and hardly had the two policemen got out and when an ambulance came alongside and the injured man was lifted on to a stretcher and driven away.

'I'd like to take down all the particulars,' one of the policemen said.

Alan glanced at Miranda. 'Do you think you could take us to the station first? I have an idea my companion is going to faint.' He put out his hands as he spoke and was just in time to catch Miranda as she crumpled.

She regained consciousness to find herself in the village police station, and was soon sitting beside an electric fire, sipping a mug of hot sweet tea.

Alan had been taken back to the scene of the accident and did not return for more than an hour, when he told her that his car was too damaged to be driven.

'Can we hire one?' she asked. 'I don't suppose there are any trains running.'

'There's no car to be hired either,' he said ruefully. 'There's only one taxi in the village and that's already halfway to London with another couple whose car broke down.'

'What bad luck!'

Alan nodded. 'It looks as if we'll have to stay here.'

'In the police station?'

'There's a hotel about a mile further on. The garage chap is waiting outside to drive us there.'

Shortly afterwards they were standing in a charmingly rustic lounge hall while Alan explained what had happened to a suitably sympathetic hotel proprietor who assured them that rooms were available and offered them coffee and biscuits while they were being prepared.

'Is there a phone I can use?' Miranda asked, wakening to the fact that Barbara would be wondering what had happened to her.

'There's a pay box behind you,' the proprietor said, and within a moment Miranda was speaking to Barbara.

'I'd better call Blaize and tell him where you are,' said Barbara. 'He's already phoned here twice.'

'What for?' Miranda asked in surprise.

'He didn't say. He called at eleven and when I said you weren't back yet, he asked me to tell you to call him as soon as you got in. He rang through half an hour ago to find out why you hadn't done so.'

Mystified as to why Blaize should want to speak to her so urgently, Miranda put down the telephone. She was half-way across the lobby when a possible answer came to mind. Did he want to tell her their engagement was over? Had he succumbed to Rosemary after all?

'Did you get through?' Alan asked from the depths of an old-fashioned settee.

She nodded, too full of chaotic thoughts to speak.

'What's wrong?' he asked. 'Feeling peculiar again?'

She was saved from replying by the arrival of the proprietress with two brandies. 'You didn't order them,' she said, 'but you both look as if you could do with them.'

Miranda took the balloon glass and sipped from it. She did not like the taste of brandy, but she knew it would do her good. If only Blaize had not seen Rosemary tonight! But even if he hadn't, it would have made no difference to the final outcome. Sooner or later his weakness would have been his undoing.

'I've asked for us to be called at seven,' Alan said. 'I'm sorry it's so early, but I have a nine-fifteen appointment at the Bank.'

'I'll be up long before then,' she assured him. 'I never sleep well in a strange bed.'

'I bet you'll sleep tonight. That brandy will have helped you to relax.'

Surprisingly Miranda did sleep well and only awoke when a maid came in with early morning tea. The kitchen did not cater for guests until eight o'clock, by which time she and Alan hoped to be well on their way, but more tea was always available, the maid told her, as well as biscuits.

Declining both, Miranda dressed hurriedly, thinking how silly evening clothes looked when seen in the morning light. Alan thought so too, for he grinned as she came down the stairs in all her finery.

'You look ready for a fancy dress party.'

'You should talk,' Miranda giggled, eyeing his dinner jacket. 'In that get-up you look like a waiter just coming off duty!'

He put his hand under her elbow and guided her out to a waiting taxi. News of the accident seemed to be common knowledge and the driver chatted about it as they drove to London, telling them how lucky they were not to have been killed.

Miranda lay back against the seat and left Alan to the conversation, only opening her eyes as the increasing drone of traffic told her they were in the suburbs.

'Do you mind if I get the driver to drop me off first?' Alan asked, glancing at his watch.

Miranda assured him she did not mind in the least, for she did not have to go to work. 'Will you be seeing Blaize?' she asked.

'Not today. He has a meeting in the West End and by the time he's through I'll be out with some clients.' The taxi stopped and he jumped out. 'I'll be in touch with you, Miranda. I'm sorry about last night.'

'It wasn't your fault,' she said.

'Well, I made sure the evening was memorable,' he said wryly, and hurried away.

Barbara was still at home when Miranda let herself into the flat, and she rushed forward to greet her like an anxious hen. 'Thank heavens you weren't injured! I wasn't sure if you were telling me the truth when you spoke to me on the telephone.'

'Did you get hold of Blaize?' Miranda asked.

'Yes, I did, and he seemed awfully put out.'

'Put out?'

'I don't think he believed me when I said you and Alan were involved in an accident.'

'Did he think we made it up?' Miranda was indignant, but seeing Barbara's expression, knew that this was exactly

170

what her friend had thought too. 'Honestly, Barbara, don't you know me better than that?'

'Who knows anybody these days?' Barbara said shamefacedly. 'You mustn't be too hard on Blaize. After all, you've led him to believe you're secretly pining for Alan.'

Miranda collapsed on to a chair. Barbara was right, and since she wanted Blaize to believe she loved Alan, it was foolish to be upset because he believed she had spent the night with him. As long as he thought this, he would not guess the truth.

'Will you tell him what happened?' Barbara asked.

'I was debating whether I should,' Miranda admitted.

'*Do*,' the older girl said. 'Pretend about the way you feel, but not about the way you are.'

'Sometimes that's a fine line of distinction,' said Miranda wryly.

'But a line, nonetheless.' Barbara stared at her. 'Would you like me to do the lunch today? You look awfully pale.'

Miranda shook her head, knowing it would be better for her to be occupied. While her bath was running she put in a call to Blaize, but he had already left for his meeting in Mayfair. Deciding not to leave her name, she hung up. She would call him later and explain what had happened. Collecting a fresh apron, she set off for the City.

CHAPTER TWELVE

MIRANDA was too busy preparing lunch for the directors of Falcon Insurance to worry why Blaize had not tried to get in touch with her again, and it was only when the entrée was served that she had time to think of him.

She was also anxious to know if Alan had telephoned the Cottage Hospital, for she kept remembering the injured man—unconscious and bleeding—on the road. How frail a human being was! Full of hope and emotion one moment, and the next destroyed by the wrong turn of a wheel. Soberly she finished tidying the kitchen and went down the steps to the street.

The sun was bright and after the dimness of the entrance hall she stood for a moment blinking in the glare. As she turned in the direction of Moorgate Station she heard her name called, but only as a car moved towards her from the other side of the street did she recognise Blaize behind the wheel. Her heart jumped in her throat. Remembering the urgency with which he had tried to contact her last night she was absolutely convinced he had come to tell her their engagement was over.

Coolly she waited at the edge of the pavement as his car drew to a stop and he leaned his head out of the window.

'I've been waiting for you for half an hour,' he said abruptly.

'You should have sent word up to me.'

He did not answer but leaned across and opened the door. 'Get in.'

Miranda flashed him a look, but his expression forbade her from commenting on his abruptness and she took her place in the front seat and watched as he pulled out into the stream of traffic, almost immediately moving out of it again to come to rest in a quiet side street. He turned off the ignition and swivelled round to face her.

'I'm waiting for an explanation, Miranda.'

'An explanation for what?'

'Last night.'

'Barbara told you.'

'Do you think I believe that nonsense?' He spoke quietly, but it was the quietness of anger held in check, and the strain of doing so was visible on his face. A muscle twitched in his cheek and his jaw was clenched, which swelled a nerve along the side of his neck. 'I want the truth,' he grated, his lips barely moving.

'You know the truth. Alan and I were involved in an accident and——'

'The car broke down,' he finished for her. 'So you had to spend the night in a hotel. If you think I'll swallow that one, you'd better think again! You planned this, didn't you? You're in love with Alan and you spent the night with him!'

Astonishment and a growing exultancy bereft her of speech. Could this be Blaize ranting at her like a jealous lover? Her exultancy grew as she saw his eyes sparking at her like pieces of flint. He was furious with jealousy and it was making him blind to the truth.

'I'm not lying to you, Blaize. We did have an accident— we were nearly killed by a drunken driver—and Alan's car was too damaged to take us to London. We had no choice but to stay the night in a hotel. In separate rooms.' She enunciated the last three words so that there could be no mistake about them.

'You spent the night with Alan,' he insisted. 'You've been angling for it. I know you only agreed to our engagement in the hope that it would make him jealous. That's why I agreed to let him take you out yesterday.'

'You *agreed*?' she cried furiously. 'What gives you the right to agree or disagree with what I do? You're not my keeper!'

'You are my fiancée.'

'And you are mine,' she retorted, 'but it didn't stop you running to have dinner with Rosemary.'

'My dinner with her was a business engagement, not a pleasurable excursion to a theatre.'

'Pleasurable?' she echoed bitterly, and then stopped. If only Blaize knew how little pleasure it had given her! 'How dare you set yourself up as my judge and jury,' she said

173

loudly. 'Put your own house in order first.'

'My house is in order.'

'So is mine—no matter what you may think to the contrary. If you don't believe me, ask Alan.'

'Do you think I would believe *him*? He's made no secret that he's attracted to you, and now he's spent the night with you——'

'Be quiet!' she exclaimed. 'Do you think we wanted to stay in a hotel in the middle of the night? We would have given anything to have been able to get back home. We had no change of clothes—no night things.' She almost choked on the words. 'You can't honestly think we planned it.'

'Not consciously, perhaps,' he admitted, 'and if there was an accident then you obviously didn't plan that. But I don't believe you couldn't get back to town. You weren't in Siberia, you know, only Sussex!'

'In a godforsaken village miles from anywhere,' she said furiously. 'You try and get a taxi to take you forty miles into town at two o'clock in the morning!'

'I darn well would have done,' he exploded, 'unless I wanted to use it as an excuse to be with you. The way Alan did.'

'It wasn't an excuse,' she cried again. 'Ask Alan yourself.'

'Do you think I'd believe him either? After all, as far as he's aware you're engaged to me.'

'I'm surprised you remember a little thing like that. One waggle from Rosemary's finger and you go running!'

'I've already told you it was a business dinner. Rosemary said——'

'Rosemary said!' she mimicked. 'Don't you have a mind of your own? Don't bother answering that,' she rushed on before he could reply. 'Where your lady love is concerned you've got as much strength of mind as a wet tissue! You should stop fighting her, Blaize. Lie down and let her walk all over you. She's probably done it already. That's why you're here, isn't it—to break off our engagement?'

'It's what you want too,' he grated. 'You can't continue the good work with Alan unless you're rid of me.'

'I don't need to try and get Alan,' she flared. 'He wants to marry me.'

'When did he say so? When he made love to you last night? When he held you in his arms and kissed you?' Blaize caught her by the shoulders and shook her as if she were a duster. Her hair tumbled about her shoulders and she tried to pull free of him.

'You're crazy!' she gasped. 'I don't know what's the matter with you. Go back to Goldilocks. I'm not your concern any more.' She began to pound him on the chest. 'I'm tired of pretending to be your fiancée. You deserve to marry Rosemary. You're a blind fool, and I won't be your guide dog any longer!' With a strength she did not know she possessed, she pulled away from his hold, simultaneously opened the door and jumped out. 'It's over!' she cried. 'Over. Go back to Rosemary. You never even left her!' Wrenching the ring off her finger, she flung it through the window on to the seat. 'Give that to your fair lady. It fits her character better than it does mine.'

'Miranda!' Blaize shouted, but she did not heed him and began to run down the street.

Ahead of her lay the entrance to the subway and she sped down the stairs to the ticket barrier. But Blaize did not follow her and she knew with appalling conviction that he never would.

Barbara was flabbergasted when Miranda recounted what had happened. 'The man is nothing but a dog in the manger,' she exclaimed. 'He doesn't want you himself, but he can't bear it when anyone else does.'

'I wouldn't say he doesn't want me,' Miranda said with candour. 'That's probably why he was annoyed. To think

175

that I'd said yes to Alan and not to *him*.'

'You never told me Blaize made a pass at you,' said Barbara.

'It wasn't exactly a pass. He was kissing me and made it obvious that he. . . . You know what I mean.'

Barbara grinned and gave Miranda a reassuring hug. 'I'm glad your phoney engagement is over. I always felt no good would come of it. Take my advice and concentrate on Alan. He would be much easier to get on with.'

'Blaize wasn't difficult,' Miranda said disconsolately. 'We never quarrelled—I mean, not a real quarrel.'

'You were always going at each other hammer and tongs.'

'We argued,' Miranda said with dignity. 'But it was usually because I provoked him.'

'Well, forget him. He's probably resting that handsome black head of his on Rosemary's bosom.'

'Now you've really made my day,' Miranda said, and burst into tears.

With an exclamation Barbara rushed to make a cup of coffee—her panacea for everything—and Miranda, sipping a cup a little later on, confessed to feeling better.

'It would never have worked with Blaize and me. I would always have been afraid that he'd go running back to Rosemary.'

'That's one fear you won't have with Alan,' said Barbara. 'I was serious about what I said before, Miranda. You should think about him seriously. Eligible males don't grow on trees.'

'And even if they did,' Miranda retorted, 'they wouldn't be left there for long!'

Barbara looked happier, seeing this comment as an indication of her friend's future plans, but Miranda, thinking of Alan later that evening, knew she could never consider him as anything other than a friend. In fact at the moment she could not contemplate loving any man except Blaize.

The telephone rang and she almost jumped out of her skin, staring at it as if it were some malevolent serpent ready to strike her. Barbara spoke into the receiver, then handed it to Miranda, mouthing Alan's name as she did so.

'Hi,' he said as Miranda spoke to him. 'I'm just calling to make sure you're none the worse for what happened last night.'

'Do you know how the man is?' she asked.

'Concussion and broken legs. I had a word with the police sergeant and he told me they'll be prosecuting him for dangerous driving.'

'He's lucky it isn't for manslaughter. We could have been killed.'

'I know,' Alan said soberly. 'We really did have a lucky escape.'

'I've had another lucky one,' she said, trying to sound flippant but not quite succeeding. 'My engagement is over.'

There was a moment of silence before Alan spoke again. 'You don't mean Blaize has finally succumbed to Rosemary?'

'I don't know and I don't care.' She gripped the receiver more firmly. 'But I don't think he's going to fight her any more.'

'I see. I thought you sounded odd when you first came on the line. What precipitated the whole thing—his dinner with Rosemary?'

'That and—and. . . .' She paused, knowing that sooner or later the full truth must be told. 'Actually Blaize thinks we spent the night together. He isn't totally convinced we were involved in the accident.'

'It's easy to prove we were,' Alan said grimly.

'Even if we did, he would still say we deliberately stayed out of town in order to——'

'If we wanted each other we wouldn't need to go to such a ridiculous subterfuge,' Alan interrupted. 'Nor would you have got engaged to him in the first place.'

'He thinks I did that to bring you up to scratch,' Miranda reminded him.

'I'd forgotten that part,' Alan said slowly. 'Well, now it's *my* turn to bring *him* to his senses. I'll go and see him.'

'I don't want him to know,' said Miranda.

'Why not?'

'Because I don't. I'd rather have him think I—that we .... it's all over with him,' she said wildly. 'Let him think what he likes.'

'What you mean is that you don't care what he thinks about you as long as he doesn't know you love him?'

'That about sums it up,' she said unhappily. 'I know it might be awkward for you if you don't tell him the truth.'

'That's an understatement,' Alan said drily. 'Blaize thinks I believe his engagement to you was genuine but that I still tried to seduce you.'

'Tell him *I* seduced you,' Miranda said recklessly.

'I can just see him swallowing that one.' Alan sounded both irritated and amused. 'You kidded Blaize you were falling in with his plans because it suited your plans—which was to make me jealous—while he kidded himself he was getting engaged to you to save himself from Rosemary.'

'He still thinks that.'

'I'm not so sure. Men are creatures of habit and if they believe something for a long time it can take them a while before they realise they have changed.'

'Blaize hasn't changed.' She knew what Alan was trying to say, but refused to consider it. To do so would be to encourage false hope. 'Blaize loves Rosemary, that's why he rang me from her house last night. He was so afraid to be alone with her when that American left that he tried to get in touch with me.'

'Did he say so?'

'Some things don't need to be said.'

Alan sighed. 'You could be right. I hate to think of her getting him, but....'

'That's why he mustn't know the truth about me,' Miranda reiterated. 'If you tell him I'll never speak to you again.'

'Putting it like that, you've got my silence for ever.'

'Good.' She was so reassured she felt weak at the knees. 'I'm free to go out with you tomorrow, if you want to see me.'

'You don't need to pay me for my silence, Miranda.' She caught her breath and he heard it. 'What I'm trying to say is that I'm quite content to bide my time with you. I know you're upset at the moment and I don't want to take advantage of you.'

'Blaize thinks you already have!'

'Lollipops to Blaize!' he snorted. 'I'll see you tomorrow.'

When Alan called to take Miranda out the following evening she deliberately refrained from asking him whether he had spoken to Blaize, but as soon as they had settled themselves in the car, Alan told her that he had.

'As a matter of fact Blaize made a point of coming and talking to *me*,' he told her. 'He wanted to tell me you'd only become engaged to him because of Rosemary and that he was delighted you were going to be happy with me.'

Miranda stared down at her lap, surprised to see her hands clutched together as though seeking help from one another. 'Did he say anything about Rosemary?' she asked.

'No, but he's seeing her tonight. She rang up while I was with him.' They slowed down for the traffic lights and Alan glanced at her. 'Are you sure you wouldn't like me to give him a hint about the way you feel?'

'Positive.'

'I wish it meant there was hope for *me*. You know how I feel about you, Miranda.'

'Don't,' she said quickly. 'Can't we just be friends?'

'You ask a lot of hot-blooded male,' he said with an ironic smile, 'but I'll do my best.'

Alan was as good as his word and for the next few weeks was an attentive and affectionate escort, his goodnight kiss always firm and warm, as if trying to show her that she was young and beautiful and could not continue to bypass life.

Miranda knew she was playing for time and hoped that eventually she would be able to look at another man—possibly even Alan—without thinking of a tall, black-haired one with a narrow sardonic face and quizzical eyes. In the middle of July her stay at Falcon Insurance ended and she was transferred to new clients who had just come to Barbara, a small but extremely select firm of stockbrokers. There were only four directors, but they each had one or two guests every day and they required an exceptionally high standard of cuisine, with money no object. It was an ideal position for an enterprising cook and Miranda was delighted. The happier she was in her job the less time it gave her to brood, and there were whole stretches of the day when she no longer thought of Blaize. The late afternoons and evenings were the worst, with three o'clock in the morning being the nadir. Then she would weep into her pillow, crying for the might-have-beens and for hopes that no longer existed.

Miranda had been with Clarence & Company a fortnight when Barbara told her the Managing Director had telephoned to say how delighted he was with the service he was being given. 'What he really wanted to tell me was that he hoped I wouldn't switch you to another of our kitchens, and I half promised I wouldn't. Is that all right with you?'

'Perfectly. I'm very happy there.' Miranda glanced at her watch, pushing back her chair. 'I must dash. One of the junior partners is flying back from Ireland and has promised to bring some lobsters with him. If I'm not there to receive them heaven knows what will happen.'

'They might go round pinching a few bottoms!' Barbara laughed. 'How are you going to prepare them?'

'Plain grilled, I think. It's the best way if they're really fresh.' Miranda ran into the bedroom to collect her bag and Barbara reached for the morning paper.

'The Merry Widow has got engaged,' she called out.

'Who?' Miranda asked, scurrying across the hall to the front door.

'Rosemary. Her engagement's announced today. Did you know she——'

'Yes,' Miranda lied, intent only on stopping Barbara from talking. 'Alan told me.' She rushed out and slammed the door behind her, then stopped dead and leaned against the wall, shaking too much to move. So Rosemary had finally won. How long had it been before Blaize had capitulated? She glanced down at her ringless hand. Was it three weeks or four weeks since she had flung her own ring back at him? Yet what did the weeks matter when it was the years ahead that were going to count? Happy, triumphant years for Rosemary; bitter, lonely ones for herself.

Like an automaton Miranda managed to get through the morning. The lobsters had been presented to her with a flourish of pride and she quickly set to work on them. There was a larger than usual number of guests today and she was asked to provide canapés with the pre-lunch drinks. Anxious to keep herself as preoccupied as possible, she made elaborate ones, using some pulverised lobster shells to give her home-made mayonnaise a subtle and unusual taste. It was so good that she noted it down to give to Barbara. She and the other girls all prided themselves on being able to come up with original dishes, and this little concoction of hers was simple to make and tasted delicious—though highly expensive because of the lobster shells. She piled pink creamy mounds on to crisp crackers and set them on a

181

silver dish, together with the more obvious canapés of caviare, foie gras and salmon.

By the time lunch proper was served Miranda was exhausted, partly with the effort of cooking a gargantuan meal but more from having to keep her unhappy thoughts at bay. She must have looked as tired as she felt, for the butler suggested she go home as soon as the sweet had been served, and that he and the other kitchen staff would prepare coffee and clear away.

Gratefully she accepted the offer and was in the cloakroom changing back into her outdoor clothes when she heard a commotion in the dining room. Peeping into the corridor, she saw several men hurrying towards the dining room.

'The doctor is coming at once,' one of them said, 'but he suggested we call an ambulance.'

'Much better to take him straight to the hospital in one of the cars,' a man from inside the dining room called in a loud voice. 'If one of you will give me a hand with him, I'll do it myself.'

There was the sound of footsteps and Miranda stepped hastily back, not wishing to be seen. By the time she had changed, all was quiet and she slipped into the kitchen to tell the butler she was going.

'What was all the commotion about?' she asked.

'One of the guests collapsed as I was serving the sweet. It was quite a shock to see. One minute he was quietly talking to Mr. Clarence and the next he changed colour, clutched at his throat slumped over the table.'

'Was he old?' Miranda asked.

'No, no. A young gentleman. He's never been here before.' Since the butler, who was well past retiring age, considered anyone below fifty as young, Miranda took it to mean that the guest had not put in an appearance in a bathchair.

'Perhaps it was a heart attack,' she said.

'It didn't look like it to me.' He gave Miranda an uncomfortable glance. 'It seemed more like food poisoning.'

Miranda clutched at the back of a chair. No more embarrassing fate could befall a cook than this. 'It can't be! Everything was perfectly fresh.'

'Mr. Clarence said it was food poisoning,' the butler said as if that settled everything. 'He asked me if any fish had been served apart from the lobster.'

'Fish?' Miranda echoed.

'That's right. But I told him there was only the lobster and the gentleman hadn't touched a bite of it.'

'Do you——' she swallowed. 'Do you happen to know the man's name?'

The butler shook his head and Miranda spun round and ran into the dining room. Some of the directors were still there with their guests and looked at her in astonishment as she rushed towards the table.

'Can you tell me who was taken ill?' she gasped. 'Was it a Mr. Jefferson?'

'Yes, it was,' said the young director who had brought her the lobsters. 'But I'm sure it doesn't have anything to do with your admirable cooking. It must have been something he ate before he came here.'

'No,' Miranda cried, wringing her hands. 'It was my fault. It was the canapés. I used the lobster shells in the mayonnaise.'

'That delicious pink stuff? I wondered what it was.' He glanced over his shoulder. 'You were wrong, John, it *was* fish.' He caught himself up and turned to Miranda. 'Oh, lord, I see what you mean. Blaize was tucking into them as hungrily as I was. It's the only time I've known anything go more quickly than caviare.'

'Where have they taken him?' She cut across the spate of words.

183

'Westminster.' He caught Miranda's arm and pushed her into a chair. 'Sit down a moment, you look as though you're going to faint.'

'I must go to the hospital. I have to see how he is.'

'Mr. Clarence has gone with him. He promised to call us the moment he had any news.' The young man made some movement behind Miranda and a glass of brandy was placed into her hand. 'Drink up. It will make you feel better.'

Miranda had no patience to drink anything. 'Why wasn't I told Blaize was coming?' she said faintly. 'If I'd known I would have sent word for him not to touch the sauce.'

'He was a last-minute guest. His meeting with Mr. Clarence went on longer than anticipated and we were delighted when he agreed to stay to lunch. Mr. Clarence knew of his allergy, but it didn't seem necessary to warn him not to eat the lobster and it never dawned on any of us that the canapés were dangerous.'

'It's all my fault!' Miranda wailed again, and jumped to her feet as a telephone rang.

It was Mr. Clarence. Blaize had been given an antihistamine injection to combat the swelling of his body and had recovered consciousness.

'So you've nothing to worry about,' the young director said to her kindly.

Knowing that if she stayed here she would disgrace herself by bursting into tears, Miranda mumbled her thanks and ran out. Once in the corridor her tears could not be held in check, nor could her impulse to see Blaize. Ignoring the lift, she raced for the stairs. A taxi was depositing a fare outside the entrance and she jumped in and told him to go to the Westminster Hospital as quickly as he could.

Assuming it to be a matter of life and death, they belted through the streets, though Miranda was too keyed up to feel any nervousness and, arriving at the hospital, she thrust

184

a pound note into his hand and ran into the foyer.

With brisk efficiency her breathless inquiry to see Blaize Jefferson brought forth a house doctor who directed her to the private wing, where she was met by a nurse.

'He's still feeling a bit sorry for himself,' the girl explained, 'but he's no longer in any danger.'

'May I see him?'

The nurse pointed to the door on her left and Miranda pushed it open and stepped inside. It was a large room filled with sunshine, but she had eyes only for the man lying in the bed. Despite his tan he was almost as pale as the unbecoming white surgical gown he was wearing.

'Oh, Blaize,' she choked, and took a hesitant step forward.

Hearing his name, Blaize opened his eyes. They were dull, almost opaque, yet as they looked at her they grew bright. 'Miranda,' he said huskily. 'What on earth are you doing here?'

'I had to make sure you were all right.'

'How did you know I was ill?'

'Because *I* made the canapés,' she cried, and suddenly found herself by the bed. 'There were lobster shells in them.'

'Lobsters!'

'The shells—I pounded them. It was a new recipe I made up.'

'Trust you,' he said grimly. 'I always knew you'd be the death of me one day.'

Tears spilled from her eyes and he jerked into a sitting position. 'For God's sake, Miranda, I was only kidding.'

'But it's true,' she said, crying all the harder. 'I could have killed you.'

'And now you're trying to drown me,' he said imperiously. 'Do stop weeping. I'm as fit as a flea. In an hour or so I'll be leaving here.'

Conscious that he was holding her by the wrist, she tried to pull away from him. Instantly he let her go and she stepped back from the bed. 'Are you sure you should leave so soon? You still look awfully pale.'

'I lost my lunch,' he said briefly, 'but that's no reason for me to stay here. I'll be happier in my flat.'

She thought instantly of Rosemary, full of dimpled concern and pillow plumping. Now that her anxiety for Blaize was ebbing it was being replaced by dislike. He was a donkey to love Rosemary and it served him right if he were ill.

'What's the matter with you now?' he said. 'You're looking at me like a ruffled hen.'

'There's nothing the matter with me.' She moved back two more steps and was by the door, its handle digging reassuringly into her back, telling her she only had to turn it in order to be free of him. 'Today has been—has been—quite momentous for you,' she said jerkily. 'A sort of life and death.'

Blaize raised an eyebrow. 'I don't follow you.'

'Well, perhaps not quite life and death, but rebirth. I mean, you are beginning again, aren't you ... with Rosemary, I mean. Your engagement was in the paper.'

Blaize sat up straighter. 'What paper?'

'I don't know. Barbara saw it. I was on my way out this morning when she told me.'

'Barbara told you I was engaged to Rosemary?'

'Yes.'

'Come here,' Blaize said flatly.

Miranda remained where she was.

'Come here,' Blaize said again, and as she still did not move, he pushed aside the bedclothes and swung his feet to the ground.

'Don't!' she cried, and rushed forward, stopping several feet short of him.

'For God's sake come here,' he said in the oddest voice she had ever heard.

Afraid he was still too shaky to stand without falling, she bridged the gap between them and went to push him back against the pillows. Immediately his hands came round her waist and pulled her back with him.

'Don't!' she cried, and tried to stand up straight. But he refused to let go and she felt his heart pounding loudly beneath hers. 'Blaize,' she pleaded. 'You mustn't get excited.'

'I can't help it when I'm holding you like this,' he said huskily.

'Then let me go.'

'And have you run away before I have a chance to grovel at your feet?' He felt her give a nervous start. 'Yes, I did say grovel. When Alan saw the announcement of Rosemary's engagement this morning he came and asked me what had happened. Like you, he was expecting me to be the lucky man.'

'Aren't you?'

'I'm the lucky man right enough,' Blaize said gravely, 'but only because I'm not her fiancé. She has some other poor devil in tow. Another South African whom she's known for several years.' His lips moved along Miranda's cheek as he spoke. 'I was waiting to hear about *your* engagement too. Every day I expected Alan to come in and tell me it was on. Then when he started questioning me this morning, I asked him what game he was playing at with you. I was furious with him for not doing the right thing.'

'You mean make an honest woman of me?' she demanded.

'Don't,' he said in a tormented tone. 'When I think of what I said to you, I could cut my throat. Can you forgive me, Miranda? Even if you say you can't, I won't let you go. I love you.'

'You fool,' she whispered.

'Because I love you?'

'Because you didn't know that I loved you.'

'So that's what Alan meant? He said he wanted to marry you but you'd turned him down.' Blaize pushed her slightly away from him but still held her. 'I was planning to come and see you tonight. I hadn't realised that in the meantime you were planning to kill me!'

'Don't!' she shuddered.

'I won't—so long as you say you'll marry me.'

She leaned close and rested her slight weight on his body. 'When did you fall in love with me?' she asked shyly.

'I'm not sure. I always found you physically exciting, but half the time you made me so furious I didn't know whether to kiss you or spank you.'

'And now?' she asked tremulously.

'And now I want to do something much more than kiss you.' He gave her a little shake. 'Get thee behind me, Satan. What will the nurse say if she comes in and finds you like this?'

'She'll be too jealous of me to say anything.' Miranda straightened, but remained beside him, her hands still clasped in his warm strong ones. His pallor had given way to a flush and he looked so handsome with his over-bright eyes and tousled black hair that her heart seemed to turn over in her breast. She believed his declaration of love, yet a faint doubt still lingered, casting a shadow over what should have been total happiness.

'Why are you looking sad?' he questioned in a gentle voice.

She longed to deny that she was, but it was not in her character to lie and, half turning away from him, she whispered Rosemary's name.

'You have nothing to fear from Rosemary,' he said firmly. 'There's no love more dead than a dead love.'

'But why did it die? You've loved her for years.'

'Because I hadn't met *you*. If she'd come back into my life a month later than she did, none of this would have happened. But I was still in the process of assessing my feelings for you, and my emotions were haywire.'

'Then you liked me a little bit during our phoney engagement?'

'More than a little bit, darling—though there were times when I could have wrung your neck. You made me see myself in perspective, and it wasn't a pretty sight. I deserved every one of your insults.'

'When I think of the horrible things I said to you,' Miranda said contritely, 'it's a wonder you ever spoke to me again.'

'You're like my allergy,' he teased, 'tormenting me for the rest of my days.' He pressed her hand to his mouth and kissed the palm. 'Wait outside for me while I get dressed. Then we'll go home together.'

Miranda bent and touched her lips to his brow. Home together. They were the two nicest words in the English dictionary.

Have you missed any of these bestselling Harlequin Romances?

Please use the attached order form to indicate your requirements.
All titles are available at 75¢ each. Offer expires March 31/77.

Please use the attached order form to indicate your requirements.
All titles are available at 75¢ each. Offer expires March 31/77.

Harlequin Reader Service

ORDER FORM

MAIL COUPON TO

Harlequin Reader Service,
M.P.O. Box 707,
Niagara Falls, New York 14302.

Canadian **SEND** Residents **TO:**

Harlequin Reader Service,
Stratford, Ont. N5A 6W4

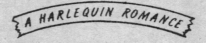
{ A HARLEQUIN ROMANCE }

Please check novels requested:

☐ 901	☐ 931	☐ 1025	☐ 1228	☐ 1369	☐ 1400	☐ 1415
☐ 904	☐ 932	☐ 1026	☐ 1230	☐ 1370	☐ 1401	☐ 1417
☐ 905	☐ 967	☐ 1030	☐ 1266	☐ 1373	☐ 1402	☐ 1418
☐ 907	☐ 973	☐ 1036	☐ 1274	☐ 1374	☐ 1403	☐ 1419
☐ 911	☐ 977	☐ 1044	☐ 1354	☐ 1376	☐ 1404	☐ 1421
☐ 913	☐ 985	☐ 1048	☐ 1356	☐ 1377	☐ 1406	☐ 1422
☐ 915	☐ 1004	☐ 1107	☐ 1357	☐ 1378	☐ 1407	☐ 1425
☐ 918	☐ 1005	☐ 1109	☐ 1358	☐ 1379	☐ 1410	☐ 1429
☐ 920	☐ 1006	☐ 1117	☐ 1360	☐ 1381	☐ 1411	☐ 1505
☐ 924	☐ 1011	☐ 1122	☐ 1362	☐ 1386	☐ 1412	
☐ 925	☐ 1013	☐ 1125	☐ 1364	☐ 1387	☐ 1413	
☐ 927	☐ 1019	☐ 1136	☐ 1366	☐ 1389	☐ 1414	

Please send me by return mail the books which I have checked.
I am enclosing 75¢ for each book ordered.

Number of books ordered _____ @ 75¢ each = $ _____

Postage and Handling = .25

TOTAL = $ _____

Name _____

Address _____

City _____

State/Prov. _____

Zip/Postal Code _____

SRP 169